Fourth Grade Is a JINX

Fourth Grade Is a JINX

Colleen O'Shaughnessy McKenna

SCHOLASTIC
HARDCOVER

Scholastic Inc.
New York

Library of Congress Cataloging-in-Publication Data

McKenna, Colleen O'Shaughnessy.
Fourth grade is a jinx / Colleen O'Shaughnessy McKenna.
p.   cm.
Summary: When fourth grader Collette sees her own mother take over
the job of teaching her class, life becomes more embarrassing and chaotic
than she can stand.

ISBN 0-590-41735-5

[1. Schools — Fiction.   2. Teacher-student relationships — Fiction.
3. Mothers and daughters — Fiction.]   I. Title.
PZ7.M478675Fo   1989
[Fic] — dc19   88-23897
                                                          CIP
                                                           AC
12 11 10 9 8 7 6 5 4 3 2   9/8 0 1 2 3 4/9

Printed in the U.S.A.   37

First Scholastic printing, April 1989

*This book is dedicated to
my mother
with thanks and love
for giving me
such a wonderful childhood*

Chapter One

"Wasn't it nice of Mrs. Johnston to let us have time in school to cover our books?" asked Collette. She opened her desk and laid her science book on top of a neatly stacked pile. "Fourth grade is going to be such a great year!"

"Great?" moaned Marsha, slumping three inches deeper in her chair. "What's so great about being forced to do all this work on the very first day of school?"

Collette looked at the clutter on Marsha's desk top and started to laugh.

"I don't see what's so funny, Collette. I still have four more books to cover, and I'm already worn out from that long math ditto we had to do this morning."

"I'll cover two books for you, Marsha."

Collette picked up a glossy cover and started to fold it over Marsha's speller.

Marsha sat up straighter and tried to smooth down her bangs. She was always pushing them straight up in the air when she got upset.

"You're so nice, Collette. Maybe you can be my best friend this year in school."

Collette tried not to frown. She bent her head over the speller and busied herself with folding and taping.

She had known Marsha for years and years, since kindergarten. They lived right across the street from each other, which is why they were friends at all.

But they certainly couldn't be called best friends. They were much, much too different from each other.

Best friends were special, almost holy. You certainly didn't call anyone your best friend unless you really meant it.

Collette looked to the back of the classroom at Sarah, her real, true, best friend. Ever since the beginning of third grade they had been close. Sarah was special. She never went out of her way

2

to get Collette mad over something, like Marsha did. In fact, Sarah was always checking to make sure Collette was having just as much fun as she was.

Sarah was an only child, just like Marsha. But she didn't go around bragging about it like it meant you were of royal blood. Marsha seemed to think the more children in a family, the less fancy the family.

Collette gave Sarah a small wave and smiled when Sarah waved back. Having a best friend in the classroom was almost as nice as being home.

"I was hoping my mom would break down and send me to Shadywood Academy this year," complained Marsha. "But here I am again, back at old fuddy-duddy Sacred Heart Elementary."

Marsha slapped her hand down on her desk and raised her eyes upward like she was praying.

"I mean, let's face it. My parents can certainly afford to send me anywhere in the city. We have money coming out of our ears!"

Looking across the desk, Collette gave a slight scowl. Maybe she didn't have as much money as Marsha, but at least she knew it was rude to talk about it.

"So I guess I'm stuck in this boring plaid uniform for another year," continued Marsha.

Collette looked down at her own uniform. She touched the small red diamond with the navy stitching of Sacred Heart printed neatly in the center.

Her jumper wasn't the least bit boring. Especially now that she was in the fourth grade and wore a size ten. Size-ten jumpers came with a pocket.

"They aren't so bad, Marsha," said Collette loyally.

She stacked Marsha's speller on top of the jumbled pile and reached for the social studies book. "Our jumpers are much nicer than the ones they wear at St. John's Academy."

"Oh, you," pouted Marsha. She blew the left side of her bangs up in the air. "You're easy to please because you don't have a million dollars' worth of clothes hanging in your closet like I do. Anyway, the plaid looks better on you with your blonde hair. But with my dark good looks, plaid makes me look drab."

Marsha made a fist and blew up the other side of her bangs. Once Marsha's forehead was show-

4

ing, you knew she was working herself up into a rage.

"Nine years old is too young to be drab!" she finally exploded.

"Marsha!" laughed Sarah as she came running over. "What are you so upset about?"

Sarah reached out and tugged gently on Collette's ponytail. Collette grinned back, glad that Sarah noticed that her hair was finally long enough for a real ponytail.

"Boy, your desk is a mess, Marsha," observed Sarah. "What have you been doing all day?"

"Everything! Come on, Sarah. Cover a book for me, please?" begged Marsha miserably. "I don't know why teachers can't cover these for us over the summer. What do they do with their time off?"

Collette and Sarah looked at each other with raised eyebrows. They tried not to smile. Once Marsha's bangs were up, she lost her temper very easily.

"If we hurry, we can go to the back of the room and get one of the free reading books," reminded Sarah. "I was helping Mrs. Johnston set them up. Boy, does she have a lot of them!"

"We never had our own library in the third

5

grade," added Collette. She held the social studies book out to Marsha. "All finished. Come on, let's go get a book before they're all taken."

"Wait for me," whined Marsha, wrestling with a wrinkled folder.

"Slow down, Marsha," said Roger. He walked slowly past her desk, balancing a book on his fingertip. "There's nothing back there for you, anyway."

Collette looked from Marsha to Roger, waiting. Roger teased all of the girls, especially Marsha, because she got the maddest the fastest.

"Why?" demanded Marsha as she tossed the last book into the jungle within her desk. "Were you rude, taking them all, Mr. Friday?"

Roger just smiled and shook his head. "No, but all the coloring books are still down in the first grade . . . where you belong."

Sarah nudged Collette lightly with her shoe and nodded toward Marsha. It was easy to see Marsha was getting ready to attack. She kept twisting a clump of hair around and around her index finger.

"Five more minutes till lunch," announced Mrs. Johnston from the front of the room.

"I just lost my appetite, thanks to Roger," muttered Marsha as she stomped back to the book-shelves.

"My dad packed my lunch this morning," said Sarah. "I can hardly wait to see what he packed me."

"Your father?" asked Collette. "Your mother is the fancy cook in your house. I thought she would make you cute little cucumber sandwiches to celebrate the first day of school."

"Not today. But my mom may end up being a famous cook. Remember that cookbook she had been working on?"

Collette nodded.

"Well, she sent it off a couple months ago and now someone in New York wants to publish it. She flew up there this morning to talk to them about stuff. She'll be gone for two days."

"New York?" Collette paused, studying Sarah's face. Was Sarah excited about her mom's book, or lonely already because her mom left for New York without her?

"Listen, Sarah, you can have half my sandwich if your dad packed you something disgusting, like sardines," offered Collette. "In fact, my mom wouldn't mind packing your whole lunch until your mom gets back. She already does three lunches — one more won't matter."

Sarah started to laugh. "Thanks, but my dad knows how to pack a lunch. I do, too, probably. Besides, my mom left lots of charts and directions about everything taped to the refrigerator."

Collette nodded, taking a step closer and lowering her voice.

"But who is going to take care of you after school, Sarah? Is your dad allowed to leave the bank early?"

Reaching down into the neck of her blouse, Sarah drew out a thin silver chain. On the end dangled a key.

"A key?" sputtered Collette. "You mean you'll . . . you'll be watching yourself?"

Sarah blushed. She shrugged her shoulders and dropped the key back down her blouse.

"It's only for an hour or two after school, Collette. I made myself some peanut butter and crackers this morning. I can eat those for a snack and read a book."

Collette nodded. What could she say? Poor Sarah! She had no idea how lonely she was going to be in her apartment. She didn't even have

8

rooms full of brothers and a little sister, like Collette.

Sarah didn't even have a dog!

"Don't mention the key to anyone," cautioned Sarah. "My parents don't want me to broadcast the fact that I'll be alone."

"Who's going to be alone?" asked Marsha as she joined them.

Sarah lifted her key.

"Oh, you lucky dog." Marsha sounded jealous. "I wish I had my own key."

"Sarah, I have a great idea," cried Collette, brightening suddenly. "Come home with me after school. Your dad could pick you up on the way from the bank. I'm sure my mother wouldn't mind you being there!"

"Mind?" interrupted Marsha. "Your house is already so crammed with little kids, your mom wouldn't even find Sarah for a day or two."

Marsha gave a smug little laugh before she reached out and snatched Sarah's arm. "Come home with me, Sarah. Since we're both *only* children, you'll feel more at home at my house. We can make popcorn in my microwave and relax in front of our VCR."

Collette sighed. Her house could never compete with Marsha's. Marsha had more fancy gadgets in her bedroom than Collette had in her whole house.

Collette still had to share a bedroom with her five-year-old sister, Laura. The two of them shared a Big Bird alarm clock.

Sarah probably thought they were Amish.

"I'll be fine," laughed Sarah. "My mom wants me to get used to this, anyway. She'll be taking more and more little trips to promote her book. She's so excited about this cookbook."

Collette took in a deep breath. Sarah was so brave, so cheerful about her mom up and leaving town.

Fourth grade must sound a whole lot older to Sarah's parents. They never left Sarah without a baby-sitter in the third grade.

"Hey, I'll call you as soon as I get home, okay, Collette?" Sarah was patting Collette's arm, whispering so Marsha wouldn't hear. "I'm used to being alone. Lots of times my parents are in the living room, reading, and I stay in my bedroom, watching T.V. or — "

"Oh, sure," Collette broke in. She tried to sound

real positive and perky. She didn't want Sarah to think she was feeling sorry for her. Besides, it wasn't as though Collette's parents were thinking about leaving Collette alone after school for hours at a time. Her mother had never had an extra key made for Collette.

Right now, there were too many little Murphys running around who needed a lot of watching. Stevie was only three, and Laura had just started kindergarten. And even though Jeff was trying to act like a cool kid all of a sudden, he was still only seven. Even cool seven-year-olds needed someone to drive them to soccer and make them a fried egg sandwich.

Looking up from her desk, Collette smiled bravely back at Sarah. There was nothing left to do now but to stand by Sarah the best way she could. That's what best friends were for.

And as soon as she got home from school she would explain things to her mother. Her mother was great at solving things. No problem was too tough for her. She would probably call Sarah's dad at the bank and cheerfully insist that Sarah come home with Collette whenever Mrs. Messland had to be out of town.

Everyone knew how much Mrs. Murphy liked kids. Sarah's dad would laugh back and say, "Sure thing. Now why didn't I think of that?"

As soon as Mrs. Johnston announced lunch, Collette stood up and smiled. Fourth grade with Mrs. Johnston was going to be a great year. Probably the best year of all!

Chapter Two

On the bus ride home, Collette sat with her brother Jeff and his best friend, Keto. Marsha sat up ahead, where she had shoved in with two sixth-grade girls.

Marsha twisted in her seat and shot Collette a smug look, pretending the girls had invited her to sit with them. Collette smiled. Both girls were staring at Marsha like she had just landed from outer space.

Marsha spent most of her life trying to get older kids to notice her.

Collette leaned her head against the cool glass, watching the trees and houses stream by. She was only half listening to Jeff and Keto talking about the huge spider they had found in a kid's locker after school.

Mostly Collette was worrying about Sarah, wondering if she were safe in her apartment, eating stale crackers all by herself.

Maybe having two younger brothers and a little sister came in handy after all. Collette's mom was so busy making sure nobody ate detergent or stuck a wet finger in an outlet that she didn't have time to sit around and think up ways to change a family.

Collette was one of the first off the bus. Marsha hung behind the drivers' seat, pointing out her fancy white house to anyone who would listen.

Collette hurried up the driveway, anxious to catch her mom alone. Well, her mother was really never alone, but sometimes she was down to one kid. That was pretty private.

"I'm home, Mom!" called Collette. She tossed her book bag on the small white bench by the door. "Mom? Where are you?"

"Down here, honey," called Mother. "Laundry room."

Running down the stairs, Collette stopped, smiling at her mother. There she was, all right, sorting socks from the dryer. Just like the old days.

"So how was your first day of school?" asked Mother.

"Wonderful. Mrs. Johnston is a new teacher and boy, is she nice. We have our own books in the class library, and she said we could bring games from home in case it rains."

"Good. Laura loves kindergarten. She already pasted stickers all over the refrigerator. She got two stickers for remembering her phone number."

From behind Mother, Collette heard a pile of towels laughing.

"What in the world was that?" asked Collette, peering behind her mother.

"I don't know," said Mother slowly. "I hope it's Stevie. His spaceship took off ten minutes ago and I haven't seen him since."

The towels giggled.

Mother tossed a knotted pair of red socks into the wicker hamper. "I hope his ship lands before dinner. We're having pizza and hot peaches."

Mother tossed two black sock balls into the basket.

"You sure do a nice job with the socks, Mom," said Collette approvingly. She picked up a pair from the basket and eyed it like a gem. It was important for her mother to feel appreciated, right here in her own laundry room.

Mother pushed back her dark hair, tucking one side behind her ear before she returned Collette's smile.

"I always did have a flare for matching socks. I minored in it in college."

Collette looked quickly around the laundry room. Surely there was something else she could compliment her mother on. Maybe if Sarah and her dad had praised Mrs. Messland more, Sarah wouldn't be alone right now.

In a corner, near the water meter, was a half-painted green dresser. Dried paint brushes, their bristles twisted into peaks, leaned wearily against the sides of an empty coffee can.

"That dresser over there sure is going to be nice when you finish it, Mom."

"*If* I ever finish it," said Mother as she leaned over her basket and reset the dryer. "I need an extra ten hours in my day, just to catch up."

"Catch up with what?"

Mother sighed and shook her head. "I wish I knew."

A muffled laugh came from the towels.

"Find me, Collette," asked the towels. "I'm hiding somewhere."

Bending down, Collette approached the towels on all fours.

"Fee, fie, foe, Feevie . . . I-SMELL-A-STEVIE!"

More laughter came from the towels, which were now backing quickly toward the wall in a rumpled heap.

"Where can that Stevie be?" Collette scratched her head and tapped her foot.

"He's gone," giggled the towels. "He isn't down here anymore."

Reaching out, Collette began to tickle the towels where a waist might be.

Stevie wiggled free from the towels, his tiny white teeth lined up in a grin as he tried to get away.

"Catch me some more, Collette," he cried as he ran out of the laundry room and into the brightly lit den.

"You better run, kid, 'cause here I come," shouted Collette.

Stevie shrieked with laughter as he raced around the chair. He turned to wave at Collette before he hopped over the coffee table and scooted back into the laundry room.

"Watch out," cried Mother, steadying the ironing board with both hands.

Stevie slid under the card table, knocking one leg up with his head.

"Watch out!" repeated Mother angrily, reaching for the stacks of folded laundry that were tumbling in an avalanche to the cement floor. "Oh, my goodness, look at this!"

Stevie darted out from under the table, running to hide behind Collette.

"Honestly!" snapped Mother as she shook each item before refolding. "Collette, you are old enough to know better. Since when do you rough-house like this indoors?"

Stevie hid his face in his hands. Finally, he peeked out from between his fingers.

"You mad, right?"

"Right," said Mother in a weary voice. "Don't run around in the house, Stevie. And Collette, well . . ."

"Sorry, Mom," said Collette quietly, bending to retrieve a sweatshirt from the floor. "I was only trying to play with him."

18

"I know," said Mother, balancing the basket on her hip. "And I appreciate that. But now that you're in the fourth grade, you should know better. You're old enough now to act a little more responsibly."

Collette cringed. Sarah's parents thought fourth grade was old enough to leave Sarah totally alone. Now it seemed that fourth grade was too old for Collette to be running around the house, having fun and . . . and . . . acting like a kid.

"So, tell me about the day," continued Mother. She grinned at Collette, letting her know that she was over being mad.

"Well, we have a new girl named Brenda. She's real pretty with blonde curly hair. She takes horseback riding lessons . . . and, oh, Mom, guess what?"

Collette's voice sounded so stricken, Mother dropped the sweatshirt she was folding.

"Sarah's mom left town!"

"She did what?"

Collette swallowed, anxious for it all to finally come out.

"Mrs. Messland found someone to publish her book, so she just hopped on a plane and left poor

Sarah all by herself. . . . She's eating crackers right now that have been on a plate all day!"

"Becky published her book!" said Mother brightly. "How wonderful!"

Collette's mouth hung open as she watched her mother getting more and more excited about the cookbook.

"But she didn't take Sarah with her, Mom. She just packed her bag, handed Sarah a key, and that was that." Collette watched her mother's face, hoping to see some sadness, maybe even anger.

"She probably didn't want to look too much like a mom in front of all those important New York publishers," added Collette. Collette's face fell as her mother started to laugh.

"It isn't funny, Mom."

"I know," said Mother with a smile. "But you are. You're such a good friend to worry about Sarah. But she'll be fine, Collette. Sarah lives in a nice, new apartment building with tight security."

"Her dad doesn't even get home until five," continued Collette. "Can't we ask him to let Sarah stay here? She's only in the fourth grade, Mom.

That isn't all that much older than third grade, you know."

"I know . . . but I am not about to tell Mr. Messland what to do with his daughter. Sarah is welcome here if it's all right with her father." Mother picked up the laundry basket and flicked off the fluorescent light with her finger. "Stevie, don't hang onto Mommy's legs like that. I'm going to trip."

"I'm going upstairs to call Sarah right now to make sure she didn't get mugged, or maybe her key didn't work in the lock . . . I hope her crackers weren't covered with bacteria!"

"Collette, she is going to be fine. Why are you getting so upset?" Mother leaned against the wall in the stairwell, giving Collette a concerned frown. "Stevie, let go of my foot, I can't walk. Don't untie my tennis shoe . . . stop that!"

"Well, if you think Sarah is so fine, maybe you'll try the same thing." Collette looked up at her mother, hoping she would deny it instantly.

"Stevie, stand up," cried Mother, shaking her left leg loose from his grip. "I am not a toy!"

Collette bit her lip, near tears. Her mother really

wasn't that happy in her laundry room, after all.

"I hope you're not planning to write a book, or — "

Mother's laugh was short. Too short to be considered a legal laugh if you really thought about it. It had the sting of a quick slap.

"I don't even have the time to *read* a book, Collette, let alone write one!"

Collette started to brighten, to smile. Her mom was funny.

She was just about to laugh when she heard her mother sigh.

It was a deep sigh, like all the air had just gone out of her mother's day.

From the bottom of the stairs, Collette watched her mom weave in and out of Stevie's path.

At the top of the stairs, Mother shifted her basket to the other hip and sighed again.

Collette frowned and shoved her hand deep into her pocket.

She didn't like this day anymore.

And she didn't like her mother sighing all the time.

A fourth grader was old enough to realize that a sigh could be a dangerous thing!

Chapter Three

Collette leaned against her school locker and studied Sarah.

"My mom brought home a half dozen bagels from New York. I'll bring you each one tomorrow for lunch," said Sarah. "Gosh, am I tired. Dad and I had to drive to the airport last night at ten o'clock."

Collette hung up her sweater and closed the locker. At least Sarah's parents didn't leave her alone in the apartment at night.

"Did she bring you something from Saks?" asked Marsha. "Not that you could wear it at this dumb school."

"No. She didn't have time to shop," answered Sarah.

"Did you give your mom back the key?" asked Collette.

Sarah shook her head. "I'll be using it again."

Collette couldn't help but look disappointed. Even though she had called Sarah after school to make sure she was all right, she had not stopped worrying about her.

"It was kind of fun being all by myself," said Sarah. She was looking right at Collette when she said it. Collette nodded her head to let Sarah know she got the message.

"Your mom is going to be so famous," squealed Marsha. "Just imagine seeing her book down at the bookstore, your mom smiling out on the cover over a big black kettle of boiling soup."

"My mom is going to buy two copies of her book," promised Collette.

"Your mom hates to cook," pointed out Marsha. "But *my* mom is going to buy ten copies, one for each member of her gourmet cooking group. Maybe your mom will want to give her a discount since she's buying so many."

"Sure," offered Sarah. "I guess."

"Class . . . class take your seats now. Michael

has something to show us," called Mrs. Johnston as she closed the classroom door.

Reaching down into a large brown bag, Michael pulled out a round ball. "I made the model of the sun while I was at my Uncle Kevin's this weekend," explained Michael as he walked to the front of the class. "It really took a long time because we used papier-mâché."

"You did a wonderful job, Michael. Class, look at the way Michael mixed the orange and red paint to create a fire effect."

"We started out with chicken wire to shape the sun," added Michael. "You can keep it, Mrs. Johnston."

Mrs. Johnston patted Michael on the shoulder and took the sun in both hands. "Let's hang it right away so we can all enjoy it."

Roger dragged a small stool over from the computer center.

"Thanks, dear." Mrs. Johnston slipped out of her heels and stepped up on the stool. "We're going to be studying space this semester. Maybe we could all make a planet, or a star."

"Our classroom would look like a real planetarium. We could put glitter on the stars," suggested Lorraine.

"Hey, listen, guys. My uncle is a security guard at Buhl Planetarium," informed Marsha. "I'm sure he would give us a huge discount if we wanted to go there on a field trip. He thinks I'm the greatest. I'm his favorite niece!"

"Then you must be his only niece," added Roger.

Mrs. Johnston looked down from the stool and frowned at Roger. "Be nice, children."

Collette watched as Mrs. Johnston double-knotted the wire. Maybe she could ask her dad to help her make a model of Saturn. She could use different-colored pipe cleaners for the rings, and —

A large black wasp flew in through the open window behind Mrs. Johnston's desk. It flew lazily around, skimming the top of everyone's head. The wasp lighted briefly on the stars of the flag before it made a beeline for Mrs. Johnston's leg.

It seemed to rest there only a second before it stung her.

"Yeow!" shrieked Mrs. Johnston. Both hands left the sun and came down to swat at the wasp.

She bent, swatted, and toppled off the stool before Collette had time to close her mouth.

"Oh, my . . . oh, my goodness," moaned Mrs. Johnston softly. Tears rose and slid out of the corners of both eyes as Mrs. Johnston struggled to sit up.

Collette stood closer to Sarah, her throat tight. She could almost feel her teacher's tears. Mrs. Johnston had to be in a lot of pain to cry right in front of a bunch of little kids who liked her so much.

"Hey . . . hey, I got stung once, Mrs. Johnston," said Roger nervously. "So . . . listen, don't worry. It only hurts for about five minutes and then you'll feel better."

Mrs. Johnston tried to smile at Roger, then stared down at her leg and shook her head.

"I think I hurt my leg when I fell. It really feels awful."

The children groaned, most taking a quick step back to give Mrs. Johnston more air.

"Could someone run down to the office for me? Tell them I need some medical help." Mrs. Johnston was whispering now, like she was afraid her own voice might wake up a fresh batch of pain.

Lorraine and Kimberly fell into each other's arms and began to sob loudly.

Marsha reached into her pocket and grabbed a small package of tissues. Rushing them up to Mrs. Johnston's side, she placed them gently on her lap.

"Here, you can keep these," she insisted. "Use all you want."

Collette looked out over the class. Everyone stood frozen.

"Come on, Sarah," said Collette quickly. "Let's go for help."

They whizzed out of the room and down past the hall monitor's small desk. They didn't even slow down to call back an explanation.

Soon the classroom was crammed with adults. They moved through the scattered groups of children, rearranging them with their paths.

"Make way, kids," ordered the gym teacher as he wheeled a stretcher in. "The medics are on the way over."

"Sit at your desks, children," called the secretary. She clapped her hands softly and sent out a smile with each nod of her head. "Let's all cooperate so Mrs. Johnston can get to the emergency room."

The gym teacher lifted Mrs. Johnston easily onto the stretcher.

Collette looked away. She glanced up at the lopsided sun, still dangling from the lights. She pinched her lips together into a tight knot, concentrating hard so she wouldn't start to cry.

How could such a terrible thing happen to such a nice teacher? Some other teacher would have just looked at Michael's sun and said, "Oh, well, thank you, Michael, but put it on the back table because we aren't even studying the sun for another six weeks."

She wouldn't have insisted on putting it up right away.

Mrs. Johnston was wheeled backward from the classroom. Her small smile appeared and disappeared with each fresh wave of pain.

The secretary, Miss Merkle, promised to stay with the children until the substitute arrived.

The hour spent in waiting seemed to fly by. Miss Merkle let the children sit on top of their desks while she told funny stories about her own life.

She even let Sarah lead a game of hangman from the board.

Miss Merkle was just about to start reading from *Tuck Everlasting* when the classroom door swung open.

The substitute stood rigidly for a good minute, her scowl framed by the doorway.

Collette blinked, watching as the sub marched in, dismissing Miss Merkle with a quick nod.

The substitute had to be about seventy or eighty years old, although she was not much taller than the children.

"I am Miss Haversham," she stated as she centered herself behind the desk. She glared at them in case anyone wanted to challenge the fact.

She dropped her large black purse into the bottom drawer and shoved it closed with the toe of her thick black shoe.

The class waited silently. Sarah looked over at Collette and carefully raised one eyebrow.

"Well, enough of this idleness," barked Miss Haversham. She walked to the front of the desk, rolling up both sleeves like she was about to carve a ham. "Your parents are not paying good tax dollars for inactivity."

30

"Miss Haversham, could we make Mrs. Johnston a get well card?" asked Michael. "I think it would make her feel better."

Collette joined with the others as they all nodded their heads.

Miss Haversham pulled a watch and chain from her pocket and studied it.

"Fine. That will give me a minute to look over the lesson-plan book."

Miss Haversham opened the rear closet and set out piles of construction paper and markers.

"Now work quickly and quietly, children . . . quickly and quietly."

Collette sat thinking before she started. She liked to map things out first when she was working with markers. After a minute she decided not to use stars or rainbows in her border. It might remind Mrs. Johnston of Michael's sun . . . and the wasp.

From across the room, Collette could see Sarah already starting to letter a verse. Sarah was really good at poetry.

Collette picked up a red marker and started to border the top, bottom, and sides of her paper with large red hearts.

In the center, in red marker, she neatly printed:

I hope you will
get well soon!
I will miss you a lot
till you're back
in the room!
Love,
Collette Murphy

"Yuck," said Roger from behind her desk. "Why are you trying to make her even sicker with all that mushy stuff?"

Roger raised his voice an octave and read her poem aloud to the class.

The heat coming from Collette's cheeks was almost to the melting point. Boys acted allergic to anything the least bit sweet.

Roger pushed his card under her nose.

"Now this will put a real smile on her face."

Collette studied the card. Roger had drawn a picture of a foot falling off a leg. In large black letters he had printed: I HOPE YOUR LEG DOESN'T ROT!

"You are weird, Roger," announced Marsha. She peered over Collette's shoulder.

One desk away, Matthew stood and read his card. He had drawn a picture of Mrs. Johnston with her leg caught in a bear trap. Snakes and spiders circled the victim.

THINGS LOOK BAD BUT DON'T BE SAD.

Pretty soon most of the boys and some of the girls were drawing pictures of the most awful things that could possibly happen to a person's leg.

Everyone started to laugh and talk louder, like someone had suddenly declared a holiday in the classroom.

"Class . . . class, hush," called Miss Haversham from behind her desk. "Remember your manners. Remember that at this very minute, your teacher is in the hospital."

Roger limped toward the pencil sharpener. He turned and grimaced as he patted his leg.

A few of the children watching started to giggle.

"Stop acting the role of a fool, young man," snapped Miss Haversham, narrowing her eyes. "Get back to your desk."

Roger nodded, then limped past Max, who promptly stuck out his foot, tripping him.

The class laughed louder.

"My leg . . . oh, goodness, I think I broke my leg," moaned Roger from the floor. He lay still for a minute, then flopped over and lay on his back, one leg sticking straight up in the air.

"Too bad it wasn't your neck, Bozo," hissed Marsha from her desk.

"Young man," snapped Miss Haversham, popping up from her chair. "Get up off the floor this instant."

She dug quickly into the pocket of her blouse and retrieved her black-rimmed glasses.

She pushed them in place atop her nose with a quick thrust and hurried down the aisle.

"Get up, Mr. Smarty Pants," she shrieked as she yanked him to his feet. "Get to the corner, where we shall be well rid of you."

The silence in the room was so thick, it was hard for Collette to breathe. She watched Roger walk to the farthest corner of the room, his chin dropping an inch with each step.

With a dramatic swoop, Miss Haversham smacked her yardstick against the chalk ledge.

"Now, would anyone like to join Mr. Smarty Pants in the corner?" She turned slowly, looking deep into the eyes of everyone in the room.

Miss Haversham took a few measured steps, pausing at several desks to shrink each child with her icy gaze.

"Never . . . I repeat, NEVER . . . have I met the likes of you children. I believe that your Mrs. Johnston is a lucky little lady to have hurt her leg so she manages a vacation from all of you."

Collette cringed in her seat. Adults certainly shouldn't talk to children like that . . . especially in school, where they were expected to memorize everything a teacher said to them.

Lorraine began to whimper. Collette shot a careful, sideways look at her. Lorraine was white as a ghost. Normally she was so pale you could see her blue veins crisscrossing all over her face. But now even her veins looked white.

Lorraine's whimper grew to an ear-cracking sob.

Lorraine was a crier, and had been since first grade. Her crying usually didn't affect Collette. Lorraine was the type to cry on Veteran's Day, even though she didn't know any soldiers.

But today, it seemed like Lorraine was crying for the whole class.

Behind her Collette heard another sniff. Oh, no! Things surely couldn't get any worse in the class-room. Now even Marsha was crying!

The sniff was followed by a muffled giggle, then a hoot.

Marsha was definitely not the emotional type, unless you counted a temper.

"This lady is unreal," muttered Marsha into the back of Collette's head. She poked Collette in the back with her pencil to make sure she was paying enough attention. "She is straight out of a bad fairy tale."

Marsha poked Collette again and gave a short laugh. "What a witch!"

Miss Haversham's eyebrows shot up like jack rabbits. She peered above, then below her glasses, shoving them up and down like a periscope.

"And what is so funny, miss?" Miss Haversham and the yardstick drew closer.

Marsha leaned back in her seat, folding her hands on top of her desk.

"Nothing," she answered, her voice beginning to fade into a polite murmur.

"Well, your 'nothing' just earned you a place in the corner with your friend, miss!"

"Roger is not my friend," Marsha giggled.

Collette's mouth went absolutely dry as Miss

Haversham banged the yardstick down on top of her desk again.

"I will not tolerate a fresh mouth!" shrieked Miss Haversham to no one in particular.

Collette swallowed a groan.

What in the world was going on, anyway? Why didn't someone from the office hear the noise and come running down the hall to check on the class?

It made Collette's hands sweat to know that she was one of twenty-four little kids stuck in a classroom with someone who didn't act like she *liked* little kids.

Collette jumped as the yardstick came down against the radiator with a tinny whack.

"Now I want the rest of you children to put your noisy heads down."

Heads, suddenly turned to lead, were drawn like magnets to the desk tops.

Even Roger, his head already facing the corner, tried to wedge it in even further.

"If I see one head up, I shall be glad to introduce it to my yardstick," warned the mighty Haversham as she patrolled the aisles. She smiled proudly as she strutted, as though she had just captured a city.

From across the room, Collette could hear Lorraine sniffing loudly.

Suddenly the door opened, framing the principal, Sister Mary Elizabeth.

She scanned the room quickly, as though searching for fire, before her eyes rested on Miss Haversham.

Miss Haversham slowly dusted off her fingertips as she returned the yardstick to the chalk ledge.

"Sister, I am so glad to see you. I was just about to send for you," began Miss Haversham. "I am afraid these rude children have been very, very — "

"Scared," finished Sister Mary Elizabeth quietly. "I could hear you shouting at them all the way down the hall, Miss Haversham."

Miss Haversham's mouth opened slightly before she clamped it shut in an angry frown. Her spine stiffened, her neck reaching for some level of authority.

With a deep frown she marched to the front of the room. She yanked open the bottom desk drawer, took out her purse, and shoved it deep into her armpit.

She lowered her eyes to narrow slits and walked

slowly to the door as if she expected someone to mug her at any second.

Tossing her head upward, she announced, "I'm leaving. I will not work in a place where I do not have absolute control."

When the classroom door finally closed, Sister Mary Elizabeth turned and smiled.

Collette swallowed hard, wishing she could just go home.

"Well, children, it's been quite a morning, hasn't it?" the principal said.

Lorraine blew her nose loudly.

Marsha walked away from her corner, both hands on her hips.

"I sure am glad to see you, Sister. That sub you found was not Mary Poppins!"

Collette nodded. The substitute had been so awful that she had frozen them into a giant cube of scared little kids.

"Can I get out of this corner now?" asked Roger. "My head is beginning to grow into a point."

"So what's new about that?" Marsha shouted back.

Collette laughed along with the rest of the class. It was great knowing the class was beginning to

40

thaw, that things were finally going to be normal again.

At least Miss Haversham had not left any permanent damage.

Lorraine walked up and dumped an armload of crumpled, damp tissues into the waste can. It was a sure sign that she had finally finished crying.

"I'm sorry Miss Haversham did not work out," began Sister. "Luckily, there are always many adults at the school, all of whom look out for you."

Collette nodded quickly, glad someone had thought up such a good rule.

"Now, I will find you a brand-new substitute for tomorrow," promised Sister. "The hospital called to let us know that Mrs. Johnston did break her leg. Let us remember to pray for a speedy mend. She will be back in a week, and we can all sign her cast!"

Applause rose up from the class. An end was in sight! Only a week and Mrs. Johnston would be back.

"Don't call Miss Haversham, Sister," called out Marsha. "Not even if she promises to stay in a good mood."

Sister chuckled. "Fair enough."

"And let's hide the yardstick from now on," added Michael. "Just in case."

The class laughed again, eager to laugh at just about anything.

Sister reached over and picked up *Tuck Everlasting* from Mrs. Johnston's desk.

"Would anyone like to hear a chapter?"

Collette raised her hand as high as the others. As Sister began to read, she leaned back in her chair and smiled.

A good book always seemed like a perfect way to get rid of a bad day.

The dismissal bell rang in the middle of Chapter Three.

"Good-bye, children," Sister called from the door. "Don't worry, tomorrow there will be someone special waiting for you. Just you wait and see."

Marsha ran up and grabbed Collette's arm, pulling her down the hall to the bus.

"Boy, wasn't Horrible Haversham the grouchiest old teacher you ever saw?" Marsha shuddered all over again. "I mean, she was the meanest teacher in the whole world."

"She was mean, all right," agreed Collette. "I wonder where they found her, anyway?"

"I can hardly wait to see who is sitting behind the desk tomorrow," laughed Sarah. "I hope she's nice."

"Anyone on earth would be nicer than Miss Haversham," declared Collette with a groan.

The girls giggled as they hurried down the hall to the buses. Collette could hardly wait to tell her mom all about the day. Her mom would want to know everything.

Chapter Four

On the bus ride home, the fourth graders became instant celebrities! Everyone wanted to hear about mean old Haversham. Even the sixth and seventh graders twisted around in their seats to listen.

"I heard she escaped from a mental institution near Butler last week," reported Gail, a beautiful seventh grader who never bothered to speak to anyone below the sixth grade level.

"Did she really slap Lorraine Kimble on the back with a yardstick?" asked another.

"Listen, listen, all you guys," announced Marsha in her loudest, "look-at-me" voice. She knelt on the bus seat and clapped her hands for attention. "Haversham pushed me into a corner so hard

44

that I nearly cracked my head open."

Collette turned away to shake her head. Why on earth was Marsha bothering to exaggerate when the truth was bad enough?

"I just hope I don't start getting dizzy. My mom will rush me to the hospital right away for X rays," continued Marsha, rubbing her forehead and searching for blood. "Then we would sue Haversham for every penny she has. I mean, since my Uncle Wally supplies paper products to five or six law firms, I'm sure it wouldn't cost us a thing to sue."

Marsha paused briefly to catch her breath. "Since I'm an only child, my parents take extra good care of me."

Collette frowned as she watched Mike, a sixth grader, nod his head at Marsha like he totally agreed with her parents' concern.

When the bus stopped, Collette was practically the first one off. She rushed ahead to catch up with Jeff and Keto.

She certainly didn't want to walk home with Marsha and have to listen to her ooze about how concerned "sixth-grade-Mike" was about her head.

"Your sub sounded awful," said Jeff. "I bet you're glad they fired her."

"She sure didn't like our class," said Collette. "Fourth grade is full of surprises. Some of them awful."

Tossing her book bag on the bench next to the side door, Collette ran up the three steps leading to the hall. She could hear her mother's excited voice.

"It sounds wonderful, doesn't it? Just what I need."

Collette leaned against the kitchen counter, watching her mother smile into the receiver, nodding her head up and down.

Collette leaned over and gave her mother a quick hug. It was nice to see her mother so happy. Maybe Daddy got a huge raise.

"Yes, yes, that will be fine," added Mother. "I'll see you bright and early tomorrow, Mrs. Withers."

Mrs. Withers . . . the baby-sitter? Where was her mother going, and why wasn't she taking her?

Collette's smile slid off her face like hot butter. She slumped into a chair, propping her chin in her hand.

Oh, great! She had already been through one awful day at the hands of a rented person. Now she would have to come home from school tomorrow and find another one standing right smack-dab in her kitchen.

"No, Stevie doesn't bite anymore," continued Mother in an encouraging voice. "Things will be much easier this time. No diapers — no biting!"

Mother winked at Collette, her happy smile bigger than ever.

By the time she finally hung up the phone, Mother was practically laughing out loud.

Mother kissed Collette. "How was your day?" she asked.

"Awful. You aren't going on a trip, are you?"

Mother shook her head, about to answer, when Jeff and Keto ran into the kitchen.

"Hi, Mom, can Keto stay? His school clothes are already dirty."

"That's because you pushed me into the hedge," hooted Keto, brushing leaves from his sweater.

"Sure," said Mother, happy as ever. "Call your mother first and check with her."

"Why is Mrs. Withers coming tomorrow?" persisted Collette. "Will you be gone when I come home from school?"

A loud wail from the dining room filtered into the room.

Mother frowned as she glanced over her shoulder.

"Collette, I was sorry to hear about Mrs. Johnston," Mother said as she walked into the dining room.

"How did you know?" asked Collette, suddenly disappointed. That was going to be her big news item.

Another wail, louder than the first, drifted up from under the table.

Collette lifted the lace tablecloth. Under the table, huddled together, sat Laura and Stevie.

"What are you two doing under the table?" asked Collette.

"We are running far away, Collette," informed Laura.

Stevie clutched his rusty dump truck, nodding his agreement to the plan. "I don't like that lady!" he declared.

"What lady?" asked Collette, looking around the dining room. "What is going on?"

"Why is everyone running away from home?"

laughed Jeff. He took a giant bite out of his cookie and tossed one to Keto.

Mother sighed. She sat down on the window seat, bending her head to peer under the table.

"Laura, you and Stevie are making me feel very sad. You are making things hard, and they don't have to be. We have had baby-sitters before."

"But that was at nighttime," cried Laura. "Then I could go to bed when they came, and when I woke up, you and Daddy were back home again."

"Yeah," added Stevie. He stuck his head between the legs of the chair. "So we are leaving, right, Laura?"

Collette sat down on the floor. "Will someone tell me what is going on?"

Laura popped her wet thumb from her mouth, wiping it carefully on her shorts. She sat up straighter, ready to supply all the facts.

"Me and Stevie are sitting here, all sad, because Mommy got a job."

"A job!" squeaked Collette. She spun around to stare at her mother.

"And now we have to stay with a lady who doesn't even belong to us. When I get off my kin-

dergarten van at lunchtime I'll have to show all
my pictures to someone who isn't Mommy!"

Collette dropped to her knees, crawling under
the table to put a protective arm around little
Stevie and Laura. Surely there had to be a mistake! Her mother would never run off and get a
job without asking the family what they thought
about it. Her mother loved talking about everything.

"Did Dad lose his job?" asked Jeff. "Did he get
bounced?"

Keto snickered, trying to hide it behind his
hand.

Jeff smiled. "Maybe he could get a new job at
McGreggie's. Then he'd always give us extra
fries."

Peering up from under the table, Collette
scowled at the boys. How could they be joking at
a time like this? How could they even think about
food when a family problem was getting bigger
and bigger by the moment?

What was even worse was hearing Mother start
to laugh!

"No, Daddy did not lose his job," she said. "But
I did get one."

So it was true! But how could it be!?

"I'll be helping out in Collette's classroom for a week until Mrs. Johnston gets back."

Collette sighed, the sudden relief surging through her like floodwater. She finally understood.

Of course her mother would want to help out. She was always offering to correct papers or organize field trips. She enjoyed helping. She knew that if she showed the school how much she loved education, they would do an extra good job with her children.

Her mother knew that the new substitute teacher would need all the help she could get.

"And if you're real good for Mrs. Withers, Laura and Stevie, I'll bring you both a treat every day when I get home," promised Mother. "Every day it will be something different. And you two can make me surprise pictures."

Stevie and Laura broke into smiles, scrambling out from under the table to knock Mother over with their hugs.

"Will you bring me my own pack of gum?" asked Laura. "And maybe corn curls one day?"

Mother nodded.

"Ya-hoo," shouted Stevie, racing his truck down the rug. "I want some pretzels."

Collette smiled, glad that everyone was happy again.

"Mom, why don't you let me bring the papers home?" Collette asked, following her mother back into the kitchen. "Then you won't have to waste all that money on a baby-sitter."

Mother pushed her hair behind both ears, smiling her big smile again.

"Oh, honey, you misunderstood. I'm not going to just help. You're looking at the new fourth grade substitute teacher!"

"What?"

Collette shivered, sure that her body temperature had just dropped 40 degrees. Her mother — the teacher! Standing in front of a class with her friends?

"But you can't, Mom. You just can't!"

Mother's smile froze slightly before it completely disappeared.

"I am a certified teacher, Collette."

"You're a certified mother!" wailed Collette.

Mother turned and ran water into a pan. She clamped the metal lid with a loud clank.

"For some strange reason I thought you would be pleased, Collette. Maybe even proud that your school thought of me."

"Proud . . . pleased?" Collette choked over each word. Didn't her mother understand how awkward this was going to be? "Mom, all the kids in the class will think you're giving me A's because we're related!"

"Oh, you always get A's," pointed out Jeff as he reached for another cookie. "You study too much. You need to be an outdoor kid like me and Keto."

Both boys started to laugh. Jeff finished his milk and tossed Keto another cookie.

"I'm going to get changed. Good work, Mom," Jeff called back over his shoulder. "Now you can give me ice cream money at recess in case I forget in the morning."

Collette leaned against the wall, tears stinging her eyes. Since Jeff was so thrilled with the idea of Mom being at school, maybe she could just teach his class. Let the second grade teacher come up and teach fourth.

Collette sniffed loudly. Why couldn't the wasp have stung somebody else? Why was fourth grade turning into such a jinx?

"Could you call them back and tell them you've changed your mind?" asked Collette in a low voice. "Remind them how many kids you have at home."

"But I have not changed my mind," said Mother shortly.

Collette stared at the design of the braided rug. She trailed the entire cord from the outside to the center and back. She did not want to look up and see how mad her mother's face must be.

She could already tell by her mother's voice that she was mad.

Collette kept her head down as a single tear broke free and slowly rolled down her cheek. *Ping.* The rug soaked it up before anyone else knew it had even fallen.

She didn't want to hurt her mother's feelings, but she couldn't keep quiet about something like this. How could she possibly let her mother come into the classroom . . . *her* classroom . . . and start ordering kids around like she was in charge. Do this, class, do that, class!

How would she feel, sitting at her desk, wanting to die, when her own mother ordered Roger to put his head down on his desk for being a smart mouth, or made Marsha stand in the hall for chewing gum in science class.

What if her mother had to remind Sarah to please raise her hand if she had a question?

"You could always take an aerobic dance class if you need a change of pace," suggested Collette. She looked up, feeling a little better. Her mother loved dancing. She was always dancing with Laura and Stevie. "That's it, Mom! Marsha's mother takes Jazz Jumping down at the Plaza, twice a week. You two could ride down together."

"I do not want to take Jazz Jumping classes, Collette. I am a teacher. A very good teacher," snapped Mother. She sidestepped Collette as she banged another pan on the stove.

"I just don't think it's going to work out, that's all," continued Collette slowly. "Besides, I think it's against the law to teach your own daughter."

"No, it isn't," said Mother as she thumped a package of ground beef on the counter.

Collette opened her mouth. She closed it when she realized she had nothing to say.

"From the way you're acting, you would think that I just announced my plan to rob the City Bank."

Collette giggled, then realized her mother wasn't being funny on purpose.

Collette stared at her shoes, wishing she could shrink to the size of the pennies in her loafers.

What was so awful about *not* wanting your mother in a classroom? Everything her mother said and did would be studied by her classmates.

They would all be judging her mother, she just knew it. That would be as bad as being judged herself.

Stevie walked in the kitchen. He stared at Collette, slumped miserably on a chair.

"Are you sitting on a chair because you were bad, Collette?"

"Oh, be quiet, Stevie," snapped Collette.

"Don't take your anger out on Stevie," warned Mother in a low voice.

Stevie looked at Collette and shook his head.

"Mommy's mad at you, Collette. You better go take a nap."

Collette blinked, glad for the warm tears. She knew it was all her fault that her mother was in such a rotten mood. She knew she had changed her mother's exciting news into a problem.

But wouldn't it be lying to pretend that her

mother's teaching would be anything but awful?

How terrible it was going to be, sitting at her desk in school while her mother went on and on, telling one private family story after another.

Sure, it was interesting, even funny, when a regular teacher did it.

But his or her child wasn't sitting in the second row, wanting to die!

Collette got up and left the room. Nobody wanted her around anymore.

Sitting down at the piano, Collette tried to play. She tried, but she couldn't. Misery paralyzed her whole body, right down to her fingertips.

"It's not fair," she muttered, staring at middle C. Why didn't Marsha have a teacher for a mother?

"Dinner in ten minutes," called Mother from the kitchen. "Tacos!"

Collette sat up straighter. Dinner would put everyone back in a good mood; it always did. Taco night was almost like a party. Mom had cheese, lettuce, and sauce in tiny dishes right on the table.

Collette walked back into the kitchen. Reaching out, she gave her mother a hug.

"I love you."

"Thank you," said Mother politely before she

broke away to finish putting out the napkins.

Collette knew her mom was still mad or she would have said, "Oh, I love you, too, Sweetie-girl." But she didn't.

Looking around the kitchen, cluttered with pans and glasses on the countertops, Collette felt tired. So much of the job her mother did during the day just had to be redone. Food got eaten. Clean dishes got dirty.

Behind her she could hear the other kids hurrying down the stairs. In a minute they would flood into the kitchen, scraping chairs, reaching for milk glasses. All of them gathered around the table, waiting for mother to dish out the apple-sauce, pour the milk, serve the meat.

"Maybe you do need a little change," began Collette. She took a deep breath and a step closer to her mother. "I mean, if you're sure you really *want* to try teaching fourth grade."

Mother reached out and gave Collette a tight squeeze.

"It's going to be fun, just you wait and see."

Collette nodded, not truly able to agree.

"Hey, give me a hug, too," laughed Laura as she wrapped her arms around Mother's waist.

"Where's Dad?" asked Jeff, eyeing his father's empty place.

"Working late. Sit down, Stevie. Be careful with your milk."

"O.K. You can sit at my dad's spot, Keto," offered Jeff.

Mother set the taco platter in the center of the table and slid into her seat.

"Collette, would you say grace tonight?"

Collette bent her head, grasping both hands as tightly as she could.

" . . . from thy bounty, through Christ our Lord, Amen. . . ."

Collette kept her eyes closed, listening to the clatter of forks and plates. Now was the perfect time to add her own prayer. To pray the week would fly by without a single problem. That her mother would be wonderful, the class would be perfect, and Collette would end up having fun, after all.

Collette opened her eyes and sighed. It wasn't any use.

It would take more than a dinner prayer for all that.

It would take a miracle!

Chapter Five

"I can't believe it. I just can't believe it!" shrieked Marsha. She slid across the bus seat and poked Collette with her elbow. "My mother told me all about it last night. Your mother, the substitute."

Marsha covered her mouth as she hooted again. "This is just so unreal. I mean, your mother, teaching our class!"

Collette nodded. She kept waking up all through the night, just thinking about it.

"Tell me, what is she going to wear?" asked Marsha. "I hope she went out and bought a snappy navy-blue blazer."

"No," said Collette slowly. "She's just wearing regular clothes . . . the kind she wears for church."

"Gee, well, that's too bad. . . ." Suddenly Marsha's eyes lit up. "I can hardly wait until your mom sends Roger to the office. He won't even have to do anything wrong. She should send him for walking around wearing that dumb-looking face of his."

Marsha laughed at her own joke. "I can hardly wait. Today is going to be so neat."

"Neat?" repeated Collette. "What is so neat about my mother telling my friends what they can and cannot do? How do you think I am going to feel when she marks a big red X on my paper when I make an honest mistake?"

Collette clutched her book bag more tightly.

"I just pray everyone likes her. It would be so awful if someone threw a spitball at her." Collette paused, thinking. "At least my mom isn't a mean person."

Marsha drew her eyebrows together thoughtfully.

"Well, she is a little mean. Like when she tells me to get my feet off your coffee table. My mom said that your mom is extra picky, since your furniture has to last you a whole lot longer than most people's. My mom loves to redecorate!"

Collette shifted in her seat. It was so irritating when Marsha started reminding her about how rich her family was.

"I told her to just stick to the lesson plans that Mrs. Johnston prepared," Collette said. "I reminded her not to try to be funny."

"And tell her to go out and buy a new blazer," added Marsha. "That may help."

"Why?" asked Collette. "Mrs. Johnston is a real teacher and she doesn't wear a blazer."

"Mrs. Johnston doesn't need a blazer, Collette. She already has big glasses and wrinkly hair. She looks like a teacher. Your mother looks exactly like a mother."

The bus pulled up in the semicircle in front of the school.

"Here we are," announced Marsha, rubbing her hands together. "I can hardly wait for school to begin."

Collette yawned nervously. She wasn't a bit ready.

In a few minutes she would walk into her classroom and see her very own mother writing words on the blackboard, passing out papers, smiling . . . trying her hardest.

And what if it just wasn't good enough?

Even now her poor mother didn't realize she should be wearing a navy-blue blazer!

Sarah hurried down the hall, holding onto her ponytail as she wove in and out of the crowd.

Sarah took ballet so she always looked graceful, even when she was in a hurry.

"Look, girls, my mom French-braided my ponytail this morning so I would look extra special for Collette's mother."

Collette's hand flew up to her own hair. She had to brush it herself this morning, borrowing two little kitty-cat barrettes from Laura when she couldn't find her own. She probably looked awful. Her mother had been too busy getting herself ready, and reminding Mrs. Withers about a hundred things to fix for lunch, to worry about how Collette looked.

From the doorway of the classroom, Collette could see several children already in their seats.

They were sitting up straight and tall, not knowing if the new sub was going to be mean or nice. They weren't taking any chances.

"Look at Roger, trying to be good," snickered Sarah. "I wonder how long that's going to last."

Collette prayed it would last a week.

Marsha walked past the girls and marched to the front of the room. She had a large smirk plastered all over her face.

"Good morning, Mrs. Murphy," she practically shouted in her loud "listen-to-this" voice.

Reaching into her book bag, she pulled out a large red apple.

"An apple for the teacher!" she said as she extended it across the desk. "My father said you would get a kick out of this. You know, me bringing you an apple, just like you were a real teacher."

Mrs. Murphy smiled, taking the apple and setting it on the desk.

"Thank you, Marsha."

The morning bell rang, sending the remaining children to their seats.

Collette slid quietly into her seat, her eyes glued to the floor. She didn't want to know who was staring at her.

"Good morning," said Mrs. Murphy cheerfully. "My name is Mrs. Murphy and I will be your substitute for the rest of the week."

Michael raised his hand.

"Do you like children, Mrs. Murphy?"

Mother laughed.

"I sure do."

Roger waved his hand back and forth like someone had just plugged him in. Collette narrowed her eyes, wishing she could zap him into another time zone. What rude thing was he about to say now?

"Are you Collette Murphy's older sister?"

Collette frowned. Leave it to Roger to get the day off to a bad start.

"No, her mother. But thank you for the compliment."

"Oh, brother," muttered Marsha. "Roger is so weird."

Collette just shrugged, too relieved that Roger had not been rude.

Once reading class started, the morning went well. In fact, it went so smoothly that Collette was almost able to relax. Her mother said the same sort of teacher things that Mrs. Johnston did.

It wasn't until recess that Collette was reminded that her mother was a mother first, and a teacher second.

"Did Mommy drive little Collette to school today?" asked Jimmy. "Is it true you're teacher's pet twenty-four hours a day?"

"Oh, be quiet, Jimmy," snapped Marsha.

"Are you going to tell your mommy that the big bad boys on the playground teased you?" asked Joey. Sarah put a protective arm around Collette and stuck her tongue out at the boys. "Go find a hole, Joey, and crawl into it!"

"I don't see where your mother got you, Collette," added Roger. "She's pretty and you look like a monkey."

Marsha made a fist and shook it at Roger. "Your mother had to drive to the city dump to get you, Roger," she said.

Sarah tugged Collette away from the boys. "Don't pay any attention to them. Some boys think they're funny when they're just plain rude."

"Don't tell your mommy on us," sang Joey in a high voice.

Collette turned to frown at Joey. He was usually such a nice boy who never went out of his way to bother people like Roger and Jimmy did.

Roger probably bribed him into being a pest by promising him a couple hundred baseball cards.

Collette and the girls hopped up on the gray stone wall. They crossed their arms and glared at the boys.

"That's the only way to handle boys sometimes," Marsha commented wisely as the boys turned and left.

"I just know they will go out of their way to make my life miserable for the next week," said Collette. "And there isn't a thing I can do about it."

The recess bell rang and the children ran to form class lines. Collette slowed to a walk, watching Marsha and Sarah race ahead.

By the time she reached the side door, Collette was moving at a snail's pace.

Why should she run to get back in the classroom? What was the big hurry? Roger and his gang had probably spent the entire recess period planning something just plain awful.

It was a wonderful surprise when her mother met the children at the door with a book in her hand.

"Hi. Did you have a good lunch? I thought I would read a few more chapters of *Tuck Ever-*

lasting. We have lots of time for math, don't we?"

The children laughed, agreeing at once. Collette glanced over at Roger, hoping he would be red-faced, ashamed for even thinking about giving her mother a hard time.

Looking over at him, Collette gulped. She could have sworn that Roger was winking at her mother.

The afternoon flew by as Mrs. Murphy sat on the edge of the desk and read. The room was quiet except for the distant roar of a lawnmower and the relaxed reading of Mrs. Murphy.

Science was the last class of the day. Collette smiled as she got out her science workbook.

"All right now, class," began Mrs. Murphy. "I want you to regroup your desks for science. We have twenty-four students, which would make how many groups of four?"

"Six!" announced Michael. He was so smart, he never used scratch paper.

"Correct," agreed Mrs. Murphy as she shoved Lorraine's desk next to Jimmy's.

"Wait a minute, Mrs. Murphy," wailed Marsha, holding up both hands like a cop. "We aren't allowed to move the desks."

Everyone stopped, looking from Marsha to Mrs. Murphy.

"Our real teacher, Mrs. Johnston, said that moving desks makes too many black marks," continued Marsha, eyeing the floor critically. "She announced it the very first day."

"Mrs. Johnston won't mind," replied Mrs. Murphy coolly as she moved Marsha's desk next to Ellen's.

Collette was relieved, even grateful, when Roger moved his desk next to Michael's at breakneck speed.

"Well, don't blame me if Mrs. Johnston comes back here and has a heart attack when she finds a scraped-up floor," sighed Marsha. "This is her classroom, after all."

Mrs. Murphy smiled and nodded at Marsha. "Things are fine, Marsha. All right now, class. I want you to become detectives. I will pass a box of fossils around to each group. Try and discover which animal created the fossil. Write down your findings and pass the box to the next group. Let's see which group can get the most correct answers."

Mrs. Murphy held up a large bag of hard candy.

"You will receive a peppermint for each correct answer."

"Allllll right!" cried several children, beginning to move their desks.

"That sounds like fun, Mrs. Murphy," shouted Roger from above the noise.

Collette glared at Roger, waiting for the rude crack that had to follow. Why couldn't he just leave her mother alone? Couldn't he see that she was trying her very best?

But instead, Roger smiled at Mrs. Murphy and sat up even straighter.

Collette joined her group. Soon she was drawn into the discussion, laughing with the others as they made wild and funny guesses about the mystery animals that created the fossils.

When the dismissal bell finally cut through the noise in the classroom, the children groaned.

"Ten more minutes, please," begged Sarah from her group near the door. "We've almost finished the whole box!"

"Such hard-working detectives," laughed Mrs. Murphy. "Buses won't wait. We can finish it tomorrow."

The class broke into small groups, rearranging their desks, laughing as Mrs. Murphy walked around the room, leaving peppermints on desk tops.

Collette unwrapped her mint, watching her mom from across the room.

She was a good teacher, all right. Fun.

If all the days went this smoothly, the week would fly by. She was sure of it.

Chapter Six

Collette awoke the next morning with a terrible headache. With every cough, both hands flew to her head so it would not fall off.

She walked slowly down the hall to her parents' room.

"Mom . . . Mom, I feel awful," she croaked, tugging at her mother's quilt.

Mrs. Murphy pushed back her covers, yawning and checking the clock. She stood up, putting a cool hand on Collette's forehead.

"You are warm, Sweetie."

Collette leaned against her mother, glad she didn't have to try to convince her mom of her illness.

"I'm wearing a hole in my throat with all this coughing."

Mother fluffed up her pillows and held back the quilt. "Get in my bed, Collette. I'll get you some cough syrup before I take my shower."

Daddy rolled over and patted Collette on the arm.

"Stay home from school and get some rest today, Peanut."

Collette pulled the covers up under her chin and smiled. She was probably too old to still be called Peanut, but it had such a nice sound to it. Especially when she felt so awful.

Mother flicked on the bathroom light, got the cough syrup, and walked back across the room, holding the medicine out front like a flashlight.

"This will fix you up, Collette. I have to hurry and get the other children up and ready before I leave."

"Leave?" sputtered Collette, cough syrup dribbling from her mouth. "How can you leave when I'm sick?"

Mother took the spoon and patted Collette on the cheek. "You know I have to teach today," she replied.

"Today?" cried Collette.

"Just close your eyes and rest, sweetie. I'll be out in a minute and Mrs. Withers is coming at seven-thirty."

Collette sat up. "Aren't you going to call the school and tell them your little girl is sick . . . really sick? I think I need a throat culture."

Mother laughed. "You'll be fine, Collette. I think you need a day of rest and some cough medicine. Besides, Mrs. Withers will take good care of you." Mother smiled and closed the bathroom door.

Flopping back against the pillows, Collette frowned, pulling the quilt over her head. She would not even try to get better for a baby-sitter.

"Don't use all the hot water," called Daddy as he threw back the covers.

"You better get used to cold showers, Daddy. And cold cereal . . . cold pizza . . ." Collette mumbled slowly, letting each word fall with a thud.

"You'll feel better this evening, Peanut," assured Daddy as he walked out into the hall.

Collette rolled over, thinking. Sure, it had been a good day at school yesterday. But first days can be real easy.

The truth was, her mother belonged at home. She shouldn't be walking around a classroom, being nice and special to perfect strangers when her own kids needed her at home.

Collette shivered under the thick quilt just thinking about it. Not only was her mother leaving her, even though she was sick as a dog, with a baby-sitter . . . but worst of all, her mother was going to be alone with her fourth grade class.

There could be problems.

Her mother loved making kids laugh. She thought telling stories about family experiences was absolutely terrific.

What if her mother told the class about the time Collette accidently knocked down the baked bean display at Stumpf's Market? Or what if she bragged about the fact that Collette was completely toilet-trained by twenty months?

"Well, time to go. I'll see you this afternoon," said Mother when she had finished dressing. She bent down and gave Collette a cool kiss on her forehead.

Collette forced out two coughs to let her mother know that she was getting sicker by the minute.

"I'll call at lunch to check on you," promised

Mother as she sailed out of the room. "Love you!"

" 'Bye," said Collette shortly.

With a restless shrug, Collette leaned against the brass headboard. Downstairs, she could hear Stevie and Laura laughing.

Of course they could laugh. They didn't have to worry about Mommy broadcasting family secrets.

Collette closed her eyes. She just had to try and forget how awful the day could become. Now that she wasn't in the second row to monitor it.

She heard her parents' cars leaving the driveway, both giving a little beep in farewell. A few minutes later, the side door slammed and Jeff shouted a good-bye as he raced down the street to the bus.

Collette sighed, feeling weak and very alone. She would probably just waste away, coughing and burning up with fever.

Nobody had stayed home to make sure she got better.

"Hello," whispered Mrs. Withers from the doorway.

Collette gave a slight jump. Mrs. Withers was holding a steaming tray.

"I have a cup of lemon tea and some cinnamon toast for you, dear," the baby-sitter offered.

Collette thought about sending it back. She should just turn her head and say, "No, thank you. I don't plan on eating again."

Ever! That would get her mother back home.

Mrs. Withers would hurry downstairs, pick up the phone, and call the school as quickly as she could.

"Collette won't eat a bite, poor soul," Mrs. Withers would shout into the phone. "You better give up that job and trot yourself home, Mrs. Murphy!"

But . . . the tea did smell so good. And the cinnamon seemed to be floating in two tiny butter ponds atop the toast.

"Let me set it on the bed next to you," chirped Mrs. Withers.

"Thank you. I may try a bite or two later . . . when I stop coughing so much." Collette coughed and tried to use her best weak voice. "Maybe the tea will help."

"Hey," cried Stevie, pushing aside Mrs. Withers' wide green skirt. "How come Collette gets to sleep in Mommy's bed?"

"Leave your sister be, Stevie," warned Mrs.

Withers as she steered him toward the door. "She's sick. Why don't you help me give her a real good day?"

Stevie studied Collette, nodding his head. He didn't even start to make a fuss.

A sigh slipped out as Collette shifted in the bed. Boy, baby-sitters sure must read a lot of books to know how to handle little kids like Stevie.

By lunchtime, when Collette finally awoke from a nap, she felt well enough to watch television.

When Mrs. Withers brought in a tray of chicken noodle soup and crackers, Collette was actually hungry.

"Lookee here, Collette," said Mrs. Withers as she set the tray down. "As soon as Laura got home from kindergarten she and Stevie started to make you get well cards."

Collette studied the cards. The hearts were large and crooked, but great-looking.

"And your mother called about an hour ago. She said to tell you she is bringing home fudge delight ice cream to help your throat."

Fudge delight! Collette couldn't help but smile. It was her favorite.

But Collette erased the smile and sipped her tea.

After all, she did spend the whole day alone, fighting off strep germs while her mother raced off to school like she didn't have a sick little girl at home.

Reaching into her apron pocket, Mrs. Withers drew out a handful of butterscotch candies.

"These might help your throat some."

"Thanks, Mrs. Withers. I love butterscotch."

Mrs. Withers laughed and sat at the end of the bed. "Well, I never met a child yet who doesn't love butterscotch."

Laura knocked against the wooden doorframe.

"Can I come in now?"

"Sure, come on, Laura," said Mrs. Withers. "Collette is feeling much better now."

Mrs. Withers got up and gave Laura a gentle push inside.

"Hi, Collette," said Laura softly. "I waited a long time for you to wake up. Stevie fell asleep on the couch after lunch and I was so bored."

Collette reached out and took Laura's hand. "I was sick, but I feel much better now."

Laura looked at Collette, her lips wiggling faster and faster as her eyes filled with tears.

"I want Mommy to come home. She does puzzles with me and takes me and Stevie to playgrounds. . . ."

Scooting over, Collette made room for Laura.

"She'll be home soon. Mommy's going to teach for a few more days, that's all. That isn't too long to wait."

Laura leaned against Collette, sticking her thumb back into her mouth.

"And Mrs. Withers taught you and Stevie how to make great hearts, Laura. Wait till Mommy sees the cards you made me."

Laura sniffed. "But I want Mommy to see the cards, *now*."

Reaching into her pocket, Collette pulled out four butterscotch pieces, each wrapped in bright orange paper.

"Wow, thank you, Collette," Laura said, instantly happier.

"See, Laura, Mrs. Withers is real nice. She brought that candy to share with all of us."

Laura took two pieces and backed off the bed.

"I'll give one to Stevie, so he won't steal mine."

Collette smiled as she watched Laura race out into the hall, shouting for Stevie to come and get a surprise.

Little kids were so easy to cheer up. They didn't know that a handful of butterscotch candies couldn't even begin to solve the problem of her mom wanting to get out of the house and back into the classroom.

The small alarm clock on her dad's dresser beeped twice. It was two o'clock. The class would be in the middle of science right now.

And Mrs. Murphy was in the middle of the class.

Collette sucked hard on her butterscotch, starting to crunch nervously as she wondered how many private family stories her mother had already shared with the class.

Marsha would love the whole day, laughing and raising her hand to add another embarrassing fact or two.

By the end of the day, the entire school would know Collette Murphy still slept with a white stuffed cat, and usually got very carsick during summer vacations.

Collette shuddered. What if her mom got carried away when she heard the class laughing and told them that Collette sucked her thumb one night last spring when she was sick with the chicken pox?

Collette slowly pulled the quilt up over her eyes, trying to go back to sleep.

At least then her fears about what was going on in the classroom without her would disappear.

Chapter Seven

"Trust me, Collette, your mom didn't even mention your name once," insisted Sarah.

Both girls opened their lockers and put their lunches inside.

"She didn't let one family secret slip?" asked Collette. Sarah was such a good, trustworthy friend, she would be sure and tell Collette before a perfect stranger could walk up and tease her about it.

"No. Your mom acts like a teacher in the school." Sarah shrugged and smiled. "Yesterday Michael and I both wanted to water the plants, and your mom picked Michael. She didn't play favorites."

Sarah leaned closer and started to giggle. "And

I know your mom likes me the best."

Collette felt her spine relax. It was good to know that her mom was so professional, even without Collette in the room to help monitor.

"I don't believe it!" gasped Sarah. She squeezed Collette's elbow and started to laugh. "Look at Roger!"

Collette peeked from behind her locker door, watching as Roger zipped into the classroom carrying a handful of freshly cut flowers.

The stems were wrapped in fancy green tissue paper so you knew they didn't come from his yard.

Sarah and Collette bumped into Marsha, who was already staring with an open mouth at the door.

"What is Roger going to do with those?" asked Marsha. "We don't need to bring flowers for the May altar for months!"

"These are for you, Mrs. Murphy," stammered Roger as he thrust the flowers toward her face. "All of them."

"Thank you, Roger," cried Mrs. Murphy, smelling the flowers.

"I got them at Foodtown last night," he explained. "They have a little flower cart by the cereal section. My mom said I could get whatever I wanted as long as it didn't cost more than three bucks."

Mrs. Murphy reached for her pencil can and emptied it. "Why don't we use this as a vase? Would you mind filling it with water?"

"Great idea," shouted Roger. He stood and smiled broadly at Mrs. Murphy before he bolted out into the hall.

"Yuck," whispered Marsha as she watched Roger hurry into the boys' room. "Imagine someone as disgusting as Roger getting a crush on your mother. He even brought her flowers . . . gross. You better throw them away as soon as you get home, Collette. They're probably crawling with spider eggs."

Mrs. Murphy walked out in the hall and waved her arm. "Hurry up, children."

As Mrs. Murphy was about to close the door, Kathleen Kepper slid in. Kathleen was a sixth grader who came once a week to collect the lunch money.

Kathleen held a large leather pouch under her arm in a protective grip. She stood in the doorway, her head tilted slightly upward, refusing to look at the lowly fourth graders.

"I came for the lunch money," she announced.

Mrs. Murphy smiled. "My goodness, that leather pouch is almost as big as you are."

Kathleen tossed her head back and gave a slight frown as the class laughed. Her job was really much too important to joke about, even for a substitute teacher.

Mrs. Murphy walked over to the desk and checked the middle drawer, then the side drawers. After a puzzled look, she walked to the filing cabinet and checked each drawer.

"I saw you put the lunch money in the center desk drawer after the morning bell rang, Mrs. Murphy," said Marsha. She stood up at attention in the center aisle like she was suddenly under oath. "I remember because I noticed you had a pack of gum in your drawer and we aren't allowed to have gum in the school. Not even teachers."

"I thought I put it there, myself," said Mrs. Murphy. She pulled her chair away from the desk and took out the center drawer, laying it on the desk. She bent to peer into the vacant slot.

"Do you need any help?" asked Roger from the

doorway. He gripped the pencil can filled with yellow mums.

Kathleen tapped her foot and checked her watch as though she had a plane to catch.

"Where is the money?" asked Beth, her voice beginning to shake. "I paid for two weeks this time."

"Maybe you already sent it to the office, Mom . . . I mean . . ." Collette stammered until she finally stopped. It was getting harder and harder to act like her mother wasn't her mother.

Collette wanted to run up to the front of the class and help her mother search everywhere for the money.

Double-searching always worked at home when the car keys were lost.

"Mrs. Byrnes lost her glasses last year for a whole week," offered Sarah. "But they finally showed up in the filing cabinet."

"I don't remember sending the money to the office," muttered Mrs. Murphy as she frowned at the desk.

"The lunch money reaches the office through one person," said Kathleen in a flat, uncaring voice. "And that's me."

Collette twisted in her seat to look at Sarah. Sarah was biting her lip in a worried way.

Pretty soon the whole school would be talking about the missing lunch money. Kathleen would tell the whole sixth grade, and Marsha would be busy telling the rest of the school.

By noon, everyone would know that Mrs. Murphy didn't even know how to protect the fourth grade lunch money.

Kathleen rocked back and forth on her heels.

"I really should be going. I like to stick to my schedule."

Mrs. Murphy waved her on as her eyes glanced round and round the classroom. Collette followed her mother's eyes.

Where in the world could the money be?

The money had been there this morning — Marsha had seen it. Was somebody hiding it as some sort of a stupid joke?

Collette frowned. Why would anyone want to hide it from her mother when she tried so hard to be nice to everybody? She joked with them and read them chapters from books.

Marsha leaned forward to poke Collette in the back with her pencil. Collette shook her head, refusing to turn around. She certainly didn't want to hear Marsha's opinion about how awful things were.

Marsha said it anyway.

"I bet Roger stole the money so he could buy your mother an engagement ring."

Why wasn't her mother at home? The stolen money might seem a little exciting if her own mother wasn't right smack in the middle of it.

The day dragged by, but the money did not surface. Even the principal, Sister Mary Elizabeth, came down at lunchtime and helped search the room.

At dismissal time, Mrs. Murphy closed the classroom door.

"Class, I need your help. The money is gone. Sister and I think someone took the money as a joke."

A gasp went up from the class. What an unfunny joke.

"And I think that now the person is afraid to give it back."

Mrs. Murphy paused, looking unhappy.

"We have decided that we will have to check the lockers . . . everyone's."

The class grew perfectly silent. To have Sister check their lockers was serious. Sister was even more powerful than a policeman. She could kick you out of school for the rest of your life.

"Now, before the locker search, I am going to give that person one more chance. When the bell rings, I want you to go to your lockers. Then everyone come back in here and put your head down on your desk."

Almost everyone nodded their head, trying to show how eager they were to get things settled.

"When your bus is called, walk past my desk. If you took the money, for whatever reason, drop it on my desk. The rest of you will keep your heads down. I will wait out in the hall so you will have complete privacy."

Out in the hall everyone tried to keep their eyes on their own locker, but sideways glances were everywhere.

Everyone was waiting to see someone pull the packet of missing money from his or her locker.

Everyone's head was down when the first bus was called.

"Bus 12, Bus 36, Bus 24 . . ."

Collette closed her eyes and prayed that the

money would be on top of her mother's desk when her bus was called.

"Bus 4 . . . Bus 11 . . ."

Collette stood, holding her books close to her as she filed past the large wooden desk by the door.

"Let the money be there . . . let the money be there."

Collette scanned the desk top.

No one had returned the money. The desk top was completely empty.

Collette wanted to run to her mother, to hug her tightly and offer to stay after school to help search.

She rode the last bus. No one was going to return the money to her mother.

Marsha and Sarah squeezed in beside Collette on the bus seat.

"Someone must have stolen the money when we went up to the library this morning. Too bad your mom didn't think to lock her desk."

Collette leaned back from Marsha so she could give her a full-face scowl.

"My mom is *always* thinking. This wasn't one bit her fault."

"Of course it wasn't," said Sarah, looking a little

mad herself. "I just hope they don't make your mom pay all that money back. I bet it was over a hundred dollars."

Collette slumped deeper into her seat. "I know. This makes me so mad. My mom was a real nice teacher. She even told jokes to the class."

Sarah patted Collette gently on the arm.

"I bet she doesn't even get paid extra for being funny."

"What a terrible year. I can't believe I ever thought it was going to be fun."

The bus pulled away from the school with a jolt. Collette stared out the window, watching the familiar houses and trees whiz by. The flow of scenery was soothing.

Collette suddenly wished her bus stop was miles and miles away. It would postpone her walking into the house to find out her mother had already called to announce that the lunch money was still missing.

Collette took in a deep breath and let it out slowly. Too bad she wasn't allowed to just stay on the bus and ride forever.

Chapter Eight

"Collette, Jeff, hurry up," cried Laura as she raced down the driveway.

"Mrs. Whiskers made cookies," shouted Stevie. "Hot ones!"

Jeff darted past Collette as he ran up the driveway.

"Big deal," thought Collette. She would be willing to go back to ice-cold store-bought cookies any day if she could have her mother back home where she belonged.

"Collette, I helped Mrs. Whiskers," said Stevie, reaching up and putting his hand in hers. "I cracked up them eggs all by myself."

Collette nodded and tried to smile. Poor little

93

kid didn't even know that his mom was smack-dab in the middle of a robbery.

"Hello, dear," said Mrs. Withers. She set a glass of milk down in front of Collette. "Sit down and have some cookies. . . . Oh, my, look at the time. I promised your mother I would put the casserole in at three-thirty."

Reaching for the platter, Collette took three cookies. She may as well eat now. If her mom had to pay the lunch money back, there wouldn't be any grocery money for a long time.

"I'm going upstairs to change, Mrs. Withers. I got paint on my jumper in art class and I . . ."

But Mrs. Withers was already busy with the casserole, adding milk and stirring like mad. She wasn't interested in school news.

Upstairs, Collette unzipped her jumper and hung it on a hanger. She looked at the clock — 3:35! It was so hard waiting for her mother to get home so they could talk about the missing lunch money.

Maybe she was with the principal right now, discussing a plan.

They could have found the money in a trash can in the boiler room once all the kids left. That would be terrific! Then mother could announce the good news to the class tomorrow morning and end up a hero after all!

"Murphy Solves Mystery!" whispered Collette into her mirror.

"Oh, my stars!" came a roar from downstairs. "No! No! No!"

What was wrong?

Collette tripped over her tennis-shoe laces as she bolted from her room.

"Look at what you've gone and done! Look at this mess!"

Stevie's high-pitched cry shot up the stairwell as Collette and Jeff raced down.

"Naughty, naughty, that's what you are!" snapped Mrs. Withers. She bent over Stevie and dabbed at his noodle-covered shirt with a towel.

Stevie was sitting on the kitchen floor, an open carton of eggs beside him. Broken shells, scattered like potato chips, littered the floor.

Mrs. Withers picked up two sections of the casserole dish and kicked at the other with the tip of her shoe.

"I bet this was your mama's best dish, too. What is she going to say when she finds it all broken?"

Stevie covered his eyes and cried louder.

"Yuck, I'm not eating that tonight," said Jeff from the doorway. He stared down at the chicken-and-noodle mixture scattered on the floor.

"Me, either," added Laura. "Not even if you wash it off."

Stevie removed one hand from his eyes and peeked up at Collette.

She smiled down at him. He looked so miserable.

Collette's smile was enough for him to scramble to his feet and hide behind her.

Poor kid. Collette knew that she was probably the closest thing he had to a mother right now.

"What happened to Mommy's dish, Stevie?" Collette asked.

Stevie shook his head, a few stray noodles dropping to the floor.

"I was just trying to crack the eggs into Mommy's stew," he sobbed. "Then it would taste good, like the cookies."

"Mercy," declared Mrs. Withers. "You had no right to get into things the moment I left the room, young man."

Stevie buried his face into Collette's sweater and started a fresh batch of tears.

"What is going on? Is Stevie hurt?"

Collette turned to see her mother hurrying down the hall.

"I could hear you all the way out in the driveway!"

Mother stopped at the doorway. Her mouth fell open as she surveyed the room.

"Good grief, what happened in here?"

Mrs. Withers leaned over and tried to scrape the noodles from Stevie's jeans. He scrambled away from her and reached up for Mother.

"Stevie didn't mean to do it," said Collette quickly. "He was just trying to add a few eggs to the casserole to help out."

Mrs. Withers grunted.

"I was downstairs, getting the clothes out of the dryer, like you had asked me to, Mrs. Murphy," said Mrs. Withers. "I didn't know you had to watch this child every second of the day. I'm getting too old for this kind of work, I can tell you that!"

"Our dinner is sliding all over the floor," reported Jeff.

"I'm not eating that. Not even if you try and fix it," said Laura. "Do we have extra food?"

"One at a time, one at a time," said Mother shortly. She pulled out a chair and sat down.

Stevie climbed onto her lap and refused to look at anyone.

"Accidents happen," said Mother wearily, patting Stevie on the back.

"They happen to Stevie a lot!" added Laura in a sad voice.

"I'm a hard worker, Mrs. Murphy, you know that," announced Mrs. Withers as she poked at the mess with a handful of paper towels. "And I'm not one that likes to leave someone's dinner all over the floor. But I have a bus to catch. I still have to go home and fix my Bill his dinner."

Mother reached for her purse. She handed Mrs. Withers some money. "Of course you do. Stevie will help me clean up the rest. You go catch your bus and I'll see you tomorrow."

"Tomorrow is a new day," said Mrs. Withers, raising an eyebrow and giving Stevie a final frown.

Collette saw a small bag of pretzels sticking out of Mother's jacket. She pulled it out and reached inside for a pack of gum for Laura.

"Here, guys, Mom remembered your surprise!"

"Come on, Jeff, I'll share," said Laura happily. "Let's go outside and eat my pretzels."

Stevie slid off Mother's lap.

"I'll clean up this bad mess."

"Thanks, Stevie," said Mother. She took off her jacket and laid it across her arm.

"What am I going to do about dinner?" Mother asked. "I guess I can open a can of tuna. Oh, phooey — we're out of tuna."

"What are you going to do about the missing lunch money?" asked Collette, beginning to worry all over again.

Mother shook her head. "Let me get through this problem, first. We can talk about the money later."

Collette nodded. She wanted to talk about it now, but she wouldn't push it. Her mother sure did look tired.

"This was a rotten day, wasn't it, Mom?"

Mother gave a tired grin and nodded.

"It's a jungle out there, Collette."

Stevie looked up, smiling.

"Do you get to pet the tigers, Mommy?"

Collette and Mother laughed. Mother bent

down and kissed Stevie on top of his curls. "No —
but I get to kiss you!"

"I'll help you, Stevie," offered Collette. "Then
you can help me call Daddy. Maybe he can stop
and get hamburgers."

"Or ask him to bring home a pizza," laughed
Mother. "It's a perfect way to end this day."

"Don't worry, Mom," said Collette as she
dumped a handful of noodles in the sink. "Tomorrow will be better."

It wasn't until Mother left the room that Collette
could let her frown break through.

Unless the lunch money was found soon, things
would get much worse, much faster, than the
fourth grade could imagine.

Chapter Nine

Since Marsha was already waiting at the bus stop, Collette slowed down a little. From Marsha's silly smirk, you could just tell that she was about to say something really rude.

"Lookeee here," she shouted up the sidewalk. She dangled a brown paper bag up and down as if she were ringing a bell. "I packed my lunch today. No money, no lunchee!"

Leave it to Marsha to ruin the day before it even started.

"I'm sure the school is going to let the kids eat, even if the money is still missing, Marsha."

"I don't take chances. My mother said that if she had been responsible for that much money, she would have kept it right with her until it had been collected."

Collette looked over Marsha's head, trying to see if the bus had rounded the upper corner yet.

"My mother used to be a clerk, probably head clerk," Marsha continued. "Anyway, she was a clerk for five months at the Shop 'n' Hop store, so she's used to handling large amounts of money. She never lost a cent, not a red cent."

Collette walked away and stood near Jeff until the bus came. She was worried enough without having Marsha toss her opinions at her. Her aim was perfect.

As soon as she walked in the classroom, she heard Marsha's big mouth lecturing to Karen and Sally at the pencil sharpener.

"And in those five long months, she never lost a cent, not a red cent!"

Collette slapped her notebook down on her desk as loudly as she could. Michael and Roger looked up and laughed.

"Temper, temper," warned Roger. He gave a smirk but turned it into a halfway normal look. "Don't worry, Collette. They'll find the lunch money."

102

"Of course they will," insisted Sarah. "Any minute now."

"Maybe Horrible Haversham snuck back into the room and stole the money to get even with us," suggested Michael. "We should dust for fingerprints."

"My mom said that Mrs. Murphy did the right thing. In searching us," said Beth. "She said she was surprised, since Mrs. Murphy isn't a real teacher or anything."

"She *is* a *real* teacher," snapped Collette. "Does she look like a robot?"

"Yeah," added Sarah. "Do you think she was lying in a drawer in the office and Sister Mary Elizabeth just inflated her so she could be our sub?"

Beth's eyebrows shot up. "Well, excuse me for living, Collette and Sarah. I was trying to give your mom a compliment, for Pete's sake."

"Well, just remember that Collette's mom is a human being, too, and that she's worried the most about the money," said Sarah. She looked over at Collette and gave a forceful nod of her head. She had done a great job of sticking up for Collette and Mrs. Murphy.

"Better watch out, guys," snickered Michael. "Collette might tattle to Mommy on us. Then we will have to sit in a corner."

Collette yanked open her desk and stared inside, glad she didn't have to look at anyone for a few minutes. They were awful, everyone but Sarah. How would they like it if *their* mother were sitting behind the teacher's desk?

"Mrs. Murphy, look what I have!"

Megan Babst ran into the classroom, holding a small, elegant doll above her head. "My Uncle Richard just sent this from Japan! She even has a real silk fan and tiny slippers."

Collette smiled at the beauty of the white-faced doll.

"Thank you for bringing it in, Megan," said Mrs. Murphy. She held the doll up for the class to see. "I'll put it on the table and we can look at her more closely in social studies."

Marsha waved her hand in the air.

"My uncle sent me a real Shetland sweater from England last year. I'll bring that in tomorrow. Too bad we have to wear these dumb uniforms, or I could just wear it."

"Fine. Now, class, take out a piece of paper and number from one to ten."

Collette welcomed schoolwork. She wished she could number from one to a thousand. Then there would never be any time left over for the kids to talk about the money problem.

They all thought it was her mother's fault, she just knew it. They all thought that if *their* mother had been in charge, the whole thing would never have happened.

The morning went quickly, and it wasn't until lunchtime that the subject came up again.

"I can't believe I will have to pack my lunch for days and days," moaned Marsha as she unwrapped her sandwich. "I just know I'm chewing away on scads and scads of preservatives. If only your mother hadn't lost the lunch money."

"We all wish that," replied Collette in an irritated voice. "Especially my *mother*. Imagine how she feels, Marsha!"

"Your mother isn't eating this baloney sandwich," snapped Marsha. "Your mother may be good at solving mysteries at your house, but she isn't going to solve this one."

Collette smacked her cheese sandwich down. "She went to college for four years to learn about teaching. I'm sure she had lots and lots of courses about solving classroom mysteries."

"Maybe she got a D in those courses," sang out Marsha with an unfriendly little smile on her face. "All I know is that my own father begged me not to wear my solid-gold-plated watch until the thief is caught, or . . ." Marsha rolled her eyes upward. "Or Mrs. Johnston returns."

Roger shot his apple down the table, knocking Marsha's elbow off the table.

"Don't worry, Marsha," he said. "I have something that will keep the classroom safe for your cheap little watch. I have a trained, ten-pound spider in my desk. He's trained to attack when I give the signal. He's better than a guard dog."

The girls drew back at the thought of it.

"He's six inches long with black, hairy legs," continued Roger. He leaned closer to Marsha and pointed a finger right in her face, all the while smiling a slow, mean smile.

"And I'm saving him for *you*, Marsha!"

Marsha leaped up and threw her sandwich at

Roger. The bread flew off, leaving a large circle of baloney sticking to Roger's sweater.

"Let's get out of here, girls," Marsha ordered, pulling on Sarah's and Collette's arms. "Roger may be contagious!"

Chapter Ten

After recess, Collette walked to her desk to get her pencils. They all needed to be sharpened. She certainly didn't want her mother to write MESSY WORK on top of her papers.

She opened her desk top and reached inside. That's when she saw it! Her hand shot away as though a small fire burned inside the desk.

With both hands, Collette slammed the desk top down.

"Watch it, Murphy!" shouted Roger from the pencil sharpener. "Cut out the noise. Can't you see I'm busy over here?"

Collette slid into her seat, lifting the desk top slighly to peek inside. It was still there . . . Megan's doll!

Megan's beautiful Japanese doll was lying on her porcelain face right smack in the middle of Collette's desk.

How in the world did Megan's doll get there? Collette looked nervously around the room. How was she supposed to get the doll out before the whole class found out?

Collette quickly closed the desk top, leaning both elbows on top.

Mrs. Murphy walked in from the hall, flicking the rest of the lights on.

"Did you all have a good lunch?" she asked cheerfully. "Come on in, people. Take your seats and get out your social studies, please."

Collette's hand shot up automatically. She would tell her mom right away before things got any worse.

"Yes?"

Collette swallowed. The classroom was quiet as they all turned to stare. All waiting.

"Never mind . . ." Collette stammered.

"Are we having a quiz?" asked Tom.

"No, not unless you really want one, Tom," laughed Mrs. Murphy. "Open your social studies books to page nine."

Collette opened her desk a crack and fished around inside for her book.

Megan waved her hand in the air. "Mrs. Murphy, you said I could pass my doll around in social studies. Should I do it now?"

"Sure, great idea, Megan," said Mrs. Murphy. She put her book on the desk and pulled down the map. "Tell us where in Japan your Uncle Richard visited."

"Hey," cried Megan, standing up suddenly and twirling around. "Where is my doll? I put her on the table."

"Look on the floor," suggested Sarah, bending down to look herself. "Maybe she fell behind it."

Collette did not join the others as they turned around. She knew where the doll was. Instead, she pressed her fingertips against the desk top, wishing she could seal it permanently.

"*Dum de dum dum!*" sang Roger, loudly, then giving an evil, high-pitched laugh. "The fourth-grade robber has struck again."

"Nonsense," said Mrs. Murphy calmly. "Now, has anyone seen Megan's doll?"

The class suddenly broke into angry whispers.

Mrs. Murphy frowned. She clapped her hands for attention.

"Settle down, class. If anyone took the doll, give it back now. I am not in the mood for any more jokes."

"My uncle sent it all the way from Japan," wailed Megan. "My mother even saved the stamps."

"We are going to find that doll!" declared Mrs. Murphy.

Collette's stomach dropped. She was in so much trouble and she didn't even know how she got there.

Her mother would find the doll, all right. When she used that tone of voice it meant she was going to win, or else!

Mrs. Murphy walked over to the first row of desks.

"Open your desks . . . now!"

Desk tops flew open, everyone eager to prove their innocence. Collette leaned her head in her hand, suddenly feeling weak with the need to explain.

Everything was going too fast!

Up and down the aisles marched Mrs. Murphy. She turned down the third aisle and stopped in front of Collette's desk.

"What's wrong, Collette? You are as white as a ghost."

Collette raised her head. If only she could just faint and be carried out the door.

"I have to talk to you, Mom. Right now."

Mrs. Murphy tapped her fingernails against the desk top.

"Let me finish the search first, Collette. Open your desk, so I can get this over with."

Collette shook her head. She just couldn't. No one was going to believe her now.

"You have to check everyone's desk," reminded Lorraine loudly. "Even relatives!"

Collette glared at Lorraine.

Mrs. Murphy reddened slightly as she moved Collette's hands and opened the desk.

Collette watched her mother's face grow pale as she reached in and pulled out the doll.

"Collette — "

"I didn't take it," cried Collette. "I found it in there after lunch."

"Why didn't you tell me?"

"Because . . . because I didn't want anyone to even see me take it out of my desk. I thought they would think I *did* take it. Then they would think I stole the lunch money, too. . . ."

Collette broke off, burying her face in her hands. She didn't care how silly she looked. This was all too terrible to be true.

Who was doing this to her?

"You know I would never steal," she cried from behind her hands.

Mrs. Murphy handed Megan the doll.

"There will be no more stealing in this classroom. No more practical jokes! Period."

"What's going to happen to Collette?" asked Megan. "I don't want her to get in trouble."

Collette sobbed harder than ever.

"Collette and I will go down and talk to Sister Mary Elizabeth after school," said Mrs. Murphy quickly. "Get out a piece of paper and number from one to ten. Number one . . . name the five Great Lakes."

"A quiz . . . thanks a lot," mumbled Michael.

Collette numbered her paper, barely able to see through her tears. Why had her mother deserted her?

Why didn't she rush over and hug her, shaking her finger at the class for even thinking that her little girl would steal?

Collette misspelled "Superior," not even caring. She deliberately missed question six. Let her mother think she didn't know how to teach social studies.

Collette handed in her quiz. She slapped it on the stack, refusing to even look at her mother.

Her mother was getting paid to be a teacher, which meant she couldn't act like a mother. Not even in an emergency.

Too bad she doesn't get a paycheck for taking care of me. Then she would defend me, Collette thought.

The rest of the afternoon dragged by. Collette stared at her book. She didn't raise her hand for one question, even though she knew every answer.

"It's almost time for the dismissal bell," announced Mrs. Murphy. "Girls may go to the rest rooms first today."

Collette stayed in her seat. She didn't want to be with anyone.

Sarah walked over and put her hand on Collette's shoulder.

"Collette, everyone knows you didn't take the doll. Megan feels awful that someone stuck it in your desk."

"*She* feels awful," snapped Collette. "Think how *I* feel!"

Looking up, she saw Sarah smile. Collette smiled back. Sarah was so good at being a best friend. She always stayed calm and said exactly the right thing.

"Why do awful things like this happen to me, Sarah?"

Sarah pulled Collette up by the arm, giving her a big smile.

"Your mom is going to solve this one. Don't worry, Collette. Come and walk down to the girls' room with me."

As soon as Collette closed the stall door, she slid the bolt and leaned her forehead against the cool metal.

What a relief it was to finally be alone. Now she could let her face droop to its saddest.

She stayed in the stall for a long time.

"Collette, are you coming?" asked Sarah as she rapped on the door. "You didn't fall in, did you?"

"Go on ahead. I'll be there in a minute," called Collette, trying to make her voice sound calm.

On the inside, Collette wanted to evaporate and rise into thin air, taking her problems with her.

"See you back in the room," called Sarah before the heavy wooden door closed.

Collette sat down, leaning her back against the wall. Things weren't going to work out; she could just feel it. Her mother wouldn't be able to find the missing lunch money or the thief who took the doll.

And if the kids thought she took the doll, they would think she took the lunch money as well. They would all think Collette stole because her mother was the teacher and she thought she could get away with it.

The kids would tell their parents, who would tell their neighbors, who would tell people in the grocery store. . . .

Everyone would know all about Collette Murphy without ever knowing she didn't take a single thing.

A final toilet flushed and the metal door banged open and shut.

With a deep sigh, Collette slowly slid the bolt open. She better go back to class before she was missed. The class might think she ran down to rob the drug store.

Rounding the corner by the sinks, Collette stopped.

Lorraine was crouched on the floor by the trash can.

"Lorraine, what's wrong?" cried Collette as she hurried closer. "Are you sick? Do you want me to go get the nurse?"

Lorraine quickly looked up, a horrified mask of fear on her face.

"I can go get my mom if you want," offered Collette.

"Leave me alone." Lorraine spat out each word as she tried to sweep paper scraps back under the umbrella of her jumper.

"What is all that?" asked Collette. Bending down, she picked up a ripped envelope. A five-dollar bill stuck out.

"Give me that!" demanded Lorraine, her voice

getting higher and higher. "Get out of here. Just get out!"

As Lorraine quickly stood, dollar bills, five-dollar bills, and shredded envelopes floated to the floor.

"Hey, you found it!" cried Collette happily. She knelt down and scooped up the money with both hands. "Was it in the girls' room the whole time?"

Lorraine stared down at the money for a long minute before she let the blue purse she had been holding drop to the floor.

Collette stared at the purse, knowing it was Lorraine's.

The girls' room was quiet, both girls listening to the steady drip coming from the last sink.

Finally Lorraine gave the blue purse a small kick, sending it closer to Collette.

"Go ahead and tell," she said quietly.

Before Collette had time to say anything, Lorraine turned and ran out into the noisy hall.

The dismissal bell rang, classroom doors opened, and the halls became filled with excited talking and laughter.

As locker doors started to slam, Collette began raking the money and envelopes toward her. As quickly as she could, she stuffed it all into the blue purse.

Her eyes darted from the floor to the door as she prayed out loud.

"Please don't let anyone come in . . . please, God. I'll never ask you for anything again for the rest of my life."

Collette stood up and stuck the last handful of envelopes into the large metal trash can by the sinks.

As she pushed the heavy wooden door open, she bent her head so no one could see her eyes as she hurried down the hall.

In ten minutes she was going to have to tell her mother and Sister Mary Elizabeth everything she knew about the stealing going on in the classroom.

How was she going to convince them she was innocent when she had Megan's doll in her desk and the missing lunch money in her hands?

Chapter Eleven

"Ready?"

Collette looked up at her mother standing next to the door. Once the buses had been called, the rest of the class had emptied quickly.

Sarah had stayed behind as long as she could. Before she ran out, she handed Collette a note.

"Read this before you have to go see Sister Mary Elizabeth," she whispered.

"Everyone knows you didn't take a thing," Sarah had written in her note. Sarah had underlined "Everyone" two times. "Call me as soon as you get home. Love, Sarah."

Collette reached inside her pocket and felt the folded note now, hoping it would act like a lucky rabbit's foot and bring her some good luck now.

"Ready, Collette?" repeated Mother, flicking off the classroom lights.

Collette stood up and grabbed her backpack, not feeling the least bit ready. Her head ached, crammed full of unanswered questions.

Why did Lorraine take the lunch money? Did she take the Japanese doll, too? Did Lorraine's family need the money for food because her dad lost his job?

Collette felt a wave of sadness. All she really knew about Lorraine was that she cried easily and a lot. Collette didn't even know if Lorraine *had* a dad.

Collette and her mother fell into step with each other as they walked down the empty hall to the office. Jeff was on the bus, heading home, listening to Marsha tell everyone that Collette Murphy was in the principal's office right now. Collette Murphy, getting busted for stealing Japanese merchandise.

"I know you didn't take the doll," said Mother quietly. "But I have to go through the proper channels, just like any regular teacher would do."

Collette cringed. Having a regular mom become a regular teacher meant that neither job would ever be the same again.

The closer Collette got to the bright lights of the office, the more she wanted to reach out and take her mother's hand.

But she didn't. It probably wasn't allowed on school property. Her mother was still getting paid to be a teacher.

"Why don't you get a fast drink at the water fountain, Collette? It might make you feel a little better."

Collette shrugged, then bent down to take a quick drink. A few ounces of water wouldn't make that much difference at this point.

Collette drank for a long time. At least it would delay what was going to happen. And what was going to happen, anyway?

"Hey, save some for your mom," laughed Mother as she gently tapped Collette's arm. "I'm not looking forward to this any more than you are."

Collette stood up, watching as her mother gave her a quick wink before they entered the office.

Collette felt a little better. At least her mother was *trying* to be motherly while still on duty.

122

"You can go right in," said Miss Merkle happily. The secretary had no idea Collette and her mother were there concerning major theft.

Collette swallowed several times, wondering if her mouth had ever been so dry. Maybe she would know what to say once Sister started asking questions.

Probably not. Everything was too confusing, and if she told the truth, she would be squealing on Lorraine.

Sister and her mother would be forced to shove her chair under a hanging bare light bulb and demand the truth, demand that Collette announce the true thief.

Mother opened the inner office door. Collette inched forward, her eyes glued to the green swirled carpet.

"Lorraine!" Mrs. Murphy sounded startled.

Collette's head shot up. She couldn't believe it. There sat Lorraine, twisting her ring around and around her finger.

Sister Mary Elizabeth stood and motioned to two yellow armchairs.

"Lorraine and I have had a long talk. She has something she wishes to say to you both."

Lorraine nodded. Tears shook free with each nod.

"I'm sorry. I took the doll, and . . . and I took the lunch money, too."

Mrs. Murphy slid into her seat. "Lorraine, I don't understand. Why would you do something like that?"

Lorraine shrugged, her eyes darting nervously around the room.

"Lorraine's mother has been ill for several weeks," explained Sister softly. "Things have been a little tense at home. She thought extra money would make things easier, but . . ."

Sister reached out and patted Lorraine's hand. "But she did have second thoughts the whole time, which is why she never took the purse home, after all."

Mrs. Murphy gave Lorraine's hair a gentle stroke. "I am proud of you for finally coming down here with the truth, Lorraine. That must have taken a lot of courage."

Lorraine and Collette both nodded at the same time.

"But why did you put the doll in *my* desk, Lorraine?" asked Collette. She tried not to sound too mad since Lorraine already looked miserable enough.

Lorraine looked down at the floor when she finally spoke.

"I took the doll and put it in your desk so people would finally stop talking about the lunch money."

"Why *my* desk?" sputtered Collette. "I've always been nice to you."

Lorraine finally looked up. She looked right at Mrs. Murphy.

"You have such a nice mom. I knew she would get you out of any trouble."

Mrs. Murphy sighed. "You caused a lot of trouble, Lorraine. Especially for Collette."

"Will I have to go to jail?"

"No!" cried Collette quickly. "I still have all the money. It's in my locker."

Mrs. Murphy turned and stared at Collette. "What?"

Lorraine shifted in her seat, looking uncomfortable. "I left it with Collette in the girls' room."

Sister stood up and smiled. "Collette, you and

your mother can go now. Lorraine's parents are on their way down. Just remember, everything is strictly confidential, understand?"

Lorraine looked relieved when Collette and her mother nodded.

Collette wanted to laugh out loud. She was so happy to have the mystery finally solved.

Looking over her shoulder, Collette remembered about Lorraine. Lorraine still looked unhappy. Things weren't solved for her. Lorraine still had as many problems as before.

But it was her own fault for stealing the money in the first place. Even if her mother was sick, she wouldn't feel any better knowing her daughter was stealing.

What a dumb thing to do!

And hiding the doll was even dumber. Collette shook her head, wondering why Lorraine would try to get her in trouble when she had always been nice to her. Putting the doll in Collette's desk had been just plain mean.

As Collette stood to leave, she started remembering more.

Like how scared she had been walking down the hall to the office to see the principal. She had been scared stiff, even with her mother by her side.

Lorraine had walked down the hall all by herself.

"Come on, Collette," said Mother. "Mrs. Withers has a bus to catch."

Lorraine was busy studying her shoes as though she were really interested in them. But her lips kept moving in and out real fast as though she were trying not to start crying all over again.

"Lorraine . . ." Collette walked right over and stood in front of her chair so Lorraine had to look up.

"I hope your mom feels better. . . . I'll see you in school tomorrow, okay?"

When Lorraine smiled, her whole face got bigger and brighter. She nodded her head twice, real quick, as if it were the best news she had ever heard.

Collette followed her mother down the stairs and out into the fresh air.

"Smells like honeysuckle," said Collette. She felt great. She could hardly wait to go home and call Sarah, just to let her know that everything was all right.

She wouldn't tell her about Lorraine being in the office. Sarah might be curious about what went on, but she was too nice to poke and dig to uncover every fact.

Sarah would just be glad to know that Collette was finally off the hook and the money had been found.

"You're a real good kid, you know that?" said Mother. She reached out and put her arm around Collette's shoulders.

"Thanks, Mom," laughed Collette. She slid her arm around her mother's waist and hugged her back.

"I guess I had a real good teacher!"

Chapter Twelve

"Holy cow, Mom, what is that awful smell?" Collette pounded down the stairs. "What is burning?"

She stood in the kitchen doorway, watching her mother frown at a smoking skillet.

"Gosh, I hope that wasn't our breakfast," Collette said, peering at the small flame.

Mother lifted a bottle and sprayed. She shook it and sprayed again.

Mother smiled as the flame shrank and died.

"Bingo!" said Mother with a pleased look on her face. "This was just a little rehearsal for the science experiment today. I thought I should practice because I was a little mixed up about the procedure."

"Mixed up? Gee, Mom, maybe you should try something easier."

What if the experiment was a big flop in front of the whole class?

Mother got a pot holder and carried the skillet over to the sink. "I didn't say it was too hard for me, Collette. The directions were vague, so I decided to rehearse, that's all."

"Hey, Mrs. Murphy . . . you got a letter," announced Daddy as he walked into the kitchen. "It's from Sacred Heart. Maybe they sent you a pink slip."

Daddy winked at Collette.

"Very funny," said Mother. She smiled and whacked Daddy on the rear end with the envelope. "Maybe this is my first paycheck. We should probably frame it."

Collette smiled. It would be terrific when her mother did cash her first paycheck. She promised everyone a banana split to celebrate.

"Listen to this," cried Mother brightly. "The school is offering me a full-time teaching job. Mrs. Giardina is going back for her master's and they need another teacher for the fifth grade."

"What?" Collette felt cold prickles of shock at the back of her neck.

"Wonderful," said Daddy, standing to read the letter again with Mother. "When would they like you to start?"

"But she isn't interested, Daddy!" cried Collette, half choking on a mouthful of cereal. "Today is her last day, she promised!"

Mother lowered the letter to glare at Collette.

"Don't tell me we are going to start this all over again. I had no idea the school would offer me a full-time position."

"Don't take it. They can't make you teach!" insisted Collette.

Daddy put his hand on Collette's shoulder. "This is your mother's decision."

"But we're a family," persisted Collette, her voice climbing to a shrill whine. "Shouldn't we talk about it, vote maybe?"

"I'm a good teacher," said Mother quietly.

"You're a better mother," shouted Collette.

"Lower your voice, Collette," ordered Daddy.

Mother slid into an empty chair beside Collette. "I will always try to be the best mother I can be.

But there is no law stating that I can't have another job as well. It certainly won't make me *less* of a mother. You should know that. My family comes first."

"Oh, sure," muttered Collette. She pushed her cereal bowl away. Great. Just when she had finally adjusted to one week of her mother teaching, she was forced to think about a whole lifetime of it.

A fat tear rolled slowly down her cheek. She didn't bother to wipe it away. Let her parents see how her heart was breaking.

Mother sat down beside Collette.

"Why are you trying to make me feel guilty about considering a full-time job? Lots of mothers work outside the home."

"But you never did before. You were the best mom in the whole world. You were better than those other moms."

"Collette, you're not making sense right now," said Daddy.

"It's sense to me," whined Collette. "Things were getting real perfect around here. Stevie doesn't yell as much . . . nobody wears diapers.

Mom even promised to drive for field trips this year."

Collette stopped. She tried to breathe deeply to get the tightness out of her voice.

"I just don't understand why you would want to change things, Mom, when they are so nice the way they are."

Mother set her coffee down.

"Maybe I need to change for me. Maybe things aren't perfect for me right now, Collette."

Collette felt a chill blast through her body. What was her mother saying? Was she trying to tell her that being a mother wasn't fun anymore?

And if it were true, what was she supposed to do? Just go and disappear?

And what about Jeff, Laura, and Stevie? The poor little guys were upstairs right now, getting dressed, brushing their teeth, all of them unaware that their mother was downstairs, bored stiff with being their mother!

Collette stood up, leaning against the door frame as Jeff and Laura walked sleepily into the room.

"Hi . . . can I have some hot chocolate, Mom?

I'm freezing." Jeff slid into his chair, rubbing his eyes.

"Sure, pour milk on your cereal, Jeff. Help Laura with hers, please."

"I want hot chocolate, too, please." Laura yawned and climbed onto Daddy's lap. "With three marshmallows."

Mother sipped her coffee and set the cup in the sink.

"Take over, Daddy. I'm going to be late if I don't get out of here."

Mother blew a kiss and ran upstairs, to get her coat.

Collette considered staying. It would probably be the last cup of anything hot she would get in this house. Once her mother started a full-time teaching job, it would be every man for himself.

Instead, she picked up her book bag and walked toward the side door.

Not even hot chocolate would slide past the huge lump of despair lodged in her throat.

" 'Bye," called out Collette. But nobody called back. They were all too busy laughing and grabbing at marshmallows to wave good-bye or remind her to zip up her jacket.

From outside, Collette studied the warm yellow square of light spilling out onto the driveway.

From the outside, things looked the same. Collette turned away and walked slowly down the driveway.

Nothing was the same. What ever happened to the good old days?

Chapter Thirteen

Collette kept the news to herself until she was at the lockers with Marsha and Sarah.

"I don't believe it!" exploded Marsha, her mouth unhinged with shock. "They actually offered *your* mother a full-time teaching job?"

"That's what I said," replied Collette miserably. "My mom got the letter this morning."

"That's terrific," said Sarah. "I like your mom."

"She's okay in her house," cried Marsha. She leaned against her locker for support. "But let's face it, she did almost lose a couple hundred bucks of lunch money. Why would the school offer *her* a job?"

"Marsha!" Sarah looked as shocked as Collette.

"Well, it's true," insisted Marsha. "My mom

136

thinks that maybe your mom bit off more than she could chew, if you know what I mean?"

"That isn't one bit true," snapped Sarah.

"My mom can chew anything she bites off," added Collette hotly.

Marsha all but yawned. "So what *did* happen in the office yesterday? You never did tell us."

Collette shoved her face closer to Marsha's. "I never will, either. It was personal and private and none of your business!"

Marsha put both hands on her hips and scowled back at Collette.

"And anyway, Marsha," continued Collette, feeling lighter with each word, "being a teacher is a lot harder than what your mom does."

"Hah!" Marsha shook her head in disbelief as though Collette had just announced the world was flat. "A lot you know, Collette Murphy. My mom organizes bake sales, school flea markets, tin can collections. My mom is . . . is practically a civic leader!"

"Why doesn't she lead you out of town, then?" asked Roger quietly. "That would be a real community improvement!"

Collette looked up and gasped. There stood

Roger with slicked-down hair, wearing a navy blazer. He looked like he was in church.

"What do you know, Roger?" sneered Marsha. "I haven't seen your mom in years. She probably joined the Marines to get away from you!"

Turning to Collette, she gave a fake smile.

"And you deserve to have someone as disgusting as Roger in love with your mother!" Marsha grabbed her book bag from the floor and stomped inside the classroom.

After she left, Roger and Collette exchanged embarrassed looks.

"Marsha is just in one of her Marsha moods," laughed Sarah.

"Here, give this to your mom," said Roger quickly. He dug into his pocket and handed Collette a small white box. It was fastened with five or six rubber bands and a thick piece of black electrician's tape across them all.

"What is it?" cried Sarah. "Can we open it, Roger?"

Roger went red-faced, shaking his head. "It's just a fossil."

Collette put the box in her pocket, grabbing Sarah's arm and pushing her toward the class-

138

room. She had never seen Roger so nervous before. He looked ready to explode.

"Come on, Sarah. We better hurry or we'll be late."

"Late for what?" asked Sarah, turning to stare at Collette.

Roger seemed to relax, breaking in front of both girls as he hurried into the classroom.

"Oh, Collette, grab your tennis shoes for gym," reminded Sarah. She stopped by her locker and got out her red high tops.

Collette opened her locker and sighed. She had forgotten to put on her gym shorts and they had gym first period.

"Just run down to the girls' room and put them on fast," called Sarah as she hurried into the classroom. "I want you to be on my team."

Collette nodded and walked away as fast as she dared down the hall. Any minute the bell would ring, and Sister would point to anyone still in the hall, ordering them to get back to their classrooms.

This time Sarah and Collette would be the first two in line and they would be picked to help Mrs. Smith, the gym teacher.

Marsha usually pushed her way to the front of

the line so she could help set up the relay races to the mats.

Marsha was happiest when she was in charge of things. Now she even thought she should be in charge of whether or not Mrs. Murphy took the teaching job in January.

It wasn't Marsha's decision, anyway. Wasn't her business one bit.

Collette jammed both legs into her shorts, yanking them up under her jumper. She started to frown all over again as she thought of all the rude things Marsha had been saying about her mother. It was her mother's decision. . . .

"Oh, no!" cried Collette. She glanced down at the pink ruffles hanging out of the legs of her navy-blue shorts.

"I forgot to take off my baby-doll pajama bottoms!"

Collette could hear the morning bell ringing in the hall. Collette leaned against the sink, pulling off her shorts, frowning at the pink flowered bottoms a second before she removed them, too.

"At least I still have my underwear on," muttered Collette as she dropped the bottoms on the floor and jumped back into her shorts.

As the second bell rang, Collette was hurrying down the hall. She swung open her locker door, carelessly tossed in her baby-doll pajama bottoms, and slammed the door closed.

She was panting so hard when she slid into her seat, her mother looked at her with raised eyebrows. Collette almost grinned, knowing how her mother would laugh when she heard the story.

"Take out your science notebooks," began Mrs. Murphy.

"We have gym," reminded Marsha loudly. "First period."

"We are having gym second. We switched with the sixth graders so they could leave for their field trip," explained Mrs. Murphy. She sat on the edge of her desk and looked very concerned about something.

"Class, I would like to talk to you about a very serious matter. . . ."

Collette nearly swallowed her tongue. Surely her mother wasn't going to announce she had been offered a job. Maybe even confide in them that her selfish daughter Collette didn't want her to take it.

"You never know when a fire is going to occur,"

Mrs. Murphy continued. "Sometimes the fire is so small that it is not a serious problem."

Mrs. Murphy stopped and started to laugh.

"Like last spring when our family went to a Chinese restaurant. Stevie couldn't read so he held his fortune cookie across the candle for Collette to read his fortune. Suddenly the message caught fire."

As the class began to laugh, Collette could feel her cheeks getting warmer. Roger was smiling at Mrs. Murphy and then Collette as if he could just picture the whole thing.

Even Sarah was leaning forward in her seat, a big grin on her face as she listened.

"What did Collette do?" asked Michael.

"Luckily Collette was able to drop the whole cookie into her ice water!"

The class began to laugh harder.

"But," continued Mrs. Murphy, getting off the desk. "You won't always have such a small fire. Many times the fires are larger and more dangerous. That's why it is important to learn how to make your own extinguisher."

"Cool!" cried several of the children.

"Most of the ingredients can be found in your

kitchen already. We will be using vinegar and baking soda."

Collette leaned back in her seat, crossing her fingers. She hoped this science experiment would work. She didn't want to give Marsha any more embarrassing stories to blab around the school.

"Now, let's pretend that this is a kitchen fire," began Mrs. Murphy. She lit a match and ignited a small mound of tightly rolled paper balls.

The flames shot up and out, blackening the paper balls as they shrank away from the sides of the large metal pan.

"Imagine this to be a much larger fire and we need to extinguish it before it can spread to the kitchen curtains."

Picking up a bottle, she shook it, then sprayed.

The flame went out immediately and Collette sighed with relief.

"Now I will teach you how to make a fire extinguisher."

"Hey, wait a minute." shouted Marsha from her seat. "That fire wasn't really big enough to count, Mrs. Murphy. A *real* kitchen fire would have been much bigger. I could have blown your fire out myself with one breath."

Collette made two fists, wishing she could walk over and knock Marsha one. Why did she have to add her two cents' worth to everything?

"The fire extinguisher would work on a larger fire as well, Marsha. But I didn't want to make a classroom fire large enough to be dangerous."

"That's because vinegar and baking soda can't tackle a real fire," replied Marsha smugly. "When was the last time you saw a fire engine with a big box of baking soda on the back?"

Marsha joined in with the other children as they started to laugh.

"Let's write down the ingredients and then we'll talk about the larger fire issue, Marsha." Mrs. Murphy turned and began listing the ingredients on the board. "First of all, let's remember that the baking soda . . ."

"Mrs. Murphy, quick! Fire!" shouted Roger.

Everyone broke into a noisy panic, knocking over chairs and all talking at once.

Roger backed away from the flames shooting out of the large metal trash can.

"Oh, my goodness," cried Mrs. Murphy. She dropped her chalk and raced over to the fire. "Stand back, children."

144

Flames were shooting up, some leaping almost as high as Mrs. Murphy's waist.

Mrs. Murphy grabbed the extinguisher and aimed it at the flames. Black smoke continued to rise steadily to the ceiling.

"I'm sorry," cried Roger, shoving a box of matches back into his pocket. "I just wanted to show Marsha that . . ."

"We have to get out of here now," cried Katie.

The small stream from the extinguisher was barely making a dent in the fire.

"Call the fire department!" screamed Marsha. "People can die from breathing this black smoke."

Mrs. Murphy laid the extinguisher on her desk and looked quickly around the room.

"Calm down, line up at the door," she ordered as she quickly closed the windows behind her desk.

Collette held onto her desk as the rest of the class rushed to line up. She had to stay and help her mom do something, but what?

The class quieted, watching as Mrs. Murphy reached over and grabbed the blotter from her desk. She dumped the contents on the floor in a smooth sweep as she swung it toward the fire.

Bending down, she placed the blotter across the top of the trash can.

"Oooouch!" she cried as her fingers brushed up against the hot metal can.

"Mom!" cried Collette, taking a few steps closer. What was her mother trying to do, anyway? Collette's heart was beating so fast it was surely going to burst through her jumper at any minute.

Smoke poured from the cracks between the blotter and the trash can.

Mrs. Murphy ran to the bookcase and started laying book after book on top of the blotter.

"Now the books are going to catch on fire," cried Lorraine. Her voice was at the edge of tears. "The whole classroom will ignite."

"No it won't," shouted Collette and Roger at exactly the same time.

Mrs. Murphy blew on her fingers and shook her head.

"Relax, class, it's going to be all right now."

Mrs. Murphy walked around the trash can, spraying the smoldering edges of the blotter with the fire extinguisher.

"Let's get some windows open before the fire alarm goes off," suggested Mrs. Murphy. She

146

walked down the aisle and pulled all the windows open. "Use your tablets to wave the smoke over here."

Roger put his head in his hands, leaning against the wall.

"I can't believe I did that. I am so sorry, Mrs. Murphy."

Marsha whacked Roger on the back with her tablet.

"You could have burned the whole school down, Roger."

"I just wanted to show you that Mrs. Murphy's fire extinguisher could work on any fire," snapped Roger. "If you hadn't opened your big mouth — "

"Quiet, both of you," said Mrs. Murphy sternly. She walked over and held out her hand. "I'd like the matches, Roger. We will have to talk about this during gym."

"He should get kicked out of school," pointed out Marsha. "For good!"

Mrs. Murphy crossed her arms and frowned at Marsha. "I suggest you spend a little more time with your own affairs, Marsha."

Collette drew in a breath, waiting for someone to make a face at her mom for disciplining Marsha.

But everyone was quiet. A few even smiled.

"Now, can anyone tell me why the fire finally did go out?" asked Mrs. Murphy.

Collette leaned against her desk, her legs weak. How could her mom stand there and calmly ask questions after what just happened?

"You cut off the oxygen." replied Michael. "First by closing the window, and then with the blotter. No air, no fire."

"Oh, so that's why you added the extra books to the top of the blotter," added Sarah. "So no air could sneak in."

"Exactly," said Mrs. Murphy. "What else does a fire require?"

Hands shot up.

"Fuel . . . like the paper from the trash can," said Matt. "I hope my English test was in there."

"And Roger's matches started the whole thing going," reminded Marsha. "I bet he's going to be in *big* trouble."

"Roger and I will talk about it, Marsha," said Mrs. Murphy quietly. "Now, let's take our seats and jot down a few notes about what went on here this morning."

"This fire would make a great story for the

school newspaper," said Michael. "Sixth graders still think we're pretty boring. But this was great!"

The class laughed as Mrs. Murphy rolled her eyes.

While her mother was passing out study sheets, Collette noticed how red and blistery her fingers were.

"Mom, look at your hand," whispered Collette. "Doesn't it hurt?"

Mother gave a little nod and smiled. "I'm going down to the nurse as soon as the class leaves for gym."

Mother tried to smile, but you could tell by the way she was holding the papers that her fingers must have hurt a lot.

"Fifteen more minutes," announced Mrs. Murphy. "Once your papers are completed, you may go out to your lockers and get your tennis shoes on."

"I'm already in my gym shorts," called out Marsha.

After two quick knocks on the door, it opened and a smiling boy walked in.

Everyone looked up. There stood Bradley Meyers, who was just about the biggest show-off in

149

the whole seventh grade. All the sixth and seventh grade girls were in love with him, so he thought he could be as rude as he wanted.

He was Marsha's idol.

"Yes? Can I help you?" asked Mrs. Murphy.

"Sorry to interrupt your class, Mrs. Murphy," said Bradley. He stopped and swept his smile across the room like a sprinkler. "But I found something very interesting outside your classroom. Someone in here might need them."

Then, without even cracking a smile, Bradley held up Collette's pink ruffled pajama bottoms.

As soon as the class began to roar with laughter, Collette's heart skidded to a complete stop.

Bradley jiggled the bottoms up and down like sleigh bells, making the class laugh even harder.

"Is anyone missing their bottoms?" asked Bradley in a fake sweet voice.

"They look like Roger's gym shorts to me," shouted Marsha.

Collette forced a loud laugh. She didn't want to be the only one not laughing. Then everyone would know the panties belonged to her.

As the class began to get noisier, Mrs. Murphy clapped her hands.

"Class, settle down. . . ."

Bradley held the pants even higher, like a ruffled torch. "If no one claims them, I'll have to leave them in the lost and found." Bradley waited a practiced beat before he added, "And then someone is going to be walking around with a cold rear end."

"Young man!" said Mrs. Murphy in a tightly controlled voice. "I think you have made your point."

Collette tried to steady her breathing as her mother walked quickly across the floor to Bradley.

"Sorry, but they were just lying outside by the lockers," continued Bradley, enjoying center stage. He was so used to people loving him that he had no idea how mad Mrs. Murphy was.

"I guess they just fell off someone," hooted Bradley.

The laughter was dying down as the class watched Mrs. Murphy reach Bradley's side.

Collette tried to swallow. She would die, evaporate into a thin wisp of embarrassment if her mother claimed those ruffled bottoms.

Any minute now her mother would snatch them out of Bradley's hand.

"These are Collette's lovely little panties," she would announce proudly. "She has a cute little top at home to match."

Bradley was shifting from foot to foot now, tossing the rolled-up bottoms back and forth like a tennis ball.

"So . . . what should I do with them?"

Mrs. Murphy opened the classroom door wider and shrugged.

"Put them in the lost and found, I guess."

The class giggled as Bradley nodded and turned to leave.

When Collette finally expelled the breath she had been holding, her paper lifted off her desk like a tiny carpet and sailed to the floor.

She looked up at her mother and smiled.

Mother caught Collette's eye for a brief second before she turned and started to write on the board.

"Let's try and finish up, class. We want to stay on schedule today so we will have plenty of time for our special visitor this afternoon."

"Special visitor?" cried Roger. "Don't tell me Mr. Tooth Decay is coming back to warn us about plaque again."

Mrs. Murphy laughed. "No. This visitor is very special to you all. She will be arriving on four legs instead of two."

"Mrs. Johnston!" several children shouted.

Collette felt prickles running up both arms. She remembered again how much she liked and missed Mrs. Johnston. If she was coming to visit, she must be much better.

"She'll be dropping in around two-thirty to say hello and show off her crutches," explained Mrs. Murphy. "And she will be back for good on Monday."

Collette tapped her pencil softly against the desk top, watching her mother. Was it her imagination, or did her mother sound a little sad about the announcement?

"I wish you could stay and be her assistant, Mrs. Murphy," called Sarah from the back of the room.

Twisting in her seat, Collette smiled at Sarah for being so nice to her mother.

"Yeah", "Good idea," "Me, too," joined in others.

Mrs. Murphy smiled at the class. "Thank you. I enjoyed my week with all of you. Thank you for making it so pleasant."

"Promise you will be our all-time sub, okay?"

Collette turned her head. It was Lorraine. Her face was bright red, but her eyes looked dry and happy.

"It's a deal, Lorraine," agreed Mrs. Murphy. "Now let's line up for gym."

As Collette stood up, she watched Marsha grab something from her desk and hurry to the front of the class.

"Here's another apple," said Marsha quickly, shoving it across the desk to Mrs. Murphy.

"Thank you, Marsha. Did your father send this in?"

Marsha shook her head and smiled. "No. I picked this one out. You were really good at this . . . this teaching stuff."

Collette caught her mother's eye and they both smiled at each other.

If it hadn't been so quiet in the classroom, Collette would have clapped.

Chapter Fourteen

As soon as Collette got home, she started telling the younger kids about the fire.

"And then, just when the fire was getting really bad, Mommy grabbed the desk blotter and smacked it down on top of the waste can," explained Collette. "The fire had to go out because it didn't have any more air."

Stevie frowned and squirmed closer to Collette on the couch.

"Did Mommy get burned up?"

"Of course not," assured Collette, giving Stevie a little pat. "But she did burn her fingers a little. She'll show you when she gets home."

"*If* she ever gets home," muttered Mrs. Withers.

She drew back the curtain and looked outside. "She's almost forty minutes late."

Laura tugged on Collette's sleeve. "Did Mommy cry?"

"No. She was too busy being a teacher. Teachers try not to cry in front of their students whenever possible."

Stevie nodded seriously. "My mommy is a brave mommy."

"Your mommy is also a late mommy," complained Mrs. Withers from her post at the window. She peered out from behind the curtain for the fifth time. "I've already missed the four o'clock bus, and if she doesn't hurry, I'm going to miss the four-thirty."

"She probably had to wash the boards and clean out her desk," suggested Jeff as he stretched out across the floor. "Today was her last day of teaching."

"Mrs. Johnston came in on crutches this afternoon," added Collette. "We got to sign her cast and everything. She can hardly wait to come back to teach on Monday. She really missed us."

"I missed Mommy," whispered Laura. "I'm glad today was her last day."

156

It *may* be her last day, thought Collette. Maybe her mother wanted to take the full-time teaching job after all.

Collette leaned back against the couch and watched as Jeff snuck up on Stevie. He grabbed both of Stevie's ankles and pulled him down on top of him.

"Ya-hoo," laughed Stevie, locking both arms around Jeff's middle. "Let me wrestle you, Jeff."

"Boys, watch the lamp," ordered Mrs. Withers faintly. "Now, now . . ."

She lifted the curtain and scowled out the window.

Collette scowled back. Mrs. Withers shouldn't be so mad and impatient. Didn't she listen to the story about the fire? Didn't she know what a hard job it was to teach a room full of fourth graders all day?

"My husband, Bill, sure won't like missing his dinner. He bowls tonight and I usually have his dinner on the table at four-thirty sharp, just like clockwork."

Laura looked up at Collette, worried.

"My mother will be here any minute. She never likes to be late," offered Collette.

Mrs. Withers sighed loudly, plopping down into a chair near the window. She rested her shiny black purse on top of her stomach.

"Too bad she had to pick poor Bill's bowling night to start being late," Mrs. Withers complained. "I doubt if he'll get a strike tonight, what with him being so hungry and all."

"He could make himself peanut butter and crackers," suggested Laura. "Even I know how to do that!"

Collette giggled.

"Mrs. Withers, why don't you go and catch your bus? I can watch everyone for a couple minutes till my mom gets home."

Mrs. Withers waved Collette's suggestion away like it was a pesty fly.

"Oh, shoot, you're nothing but a little kid yourself."

Collette sat up straighter. She certainly wasn't just a little kid. She was in fourth grade, which is a lot more grown up than being in third grade.

Stevie and Jeff lunged at each other, laughing as their legs and arms entwined. They began to wrestle.

"Boys," warned Mrs. Withers as she tapped her

fingers against the purse. "Watch the lamp."

"Boys!" snapped Collette. She stood up and tried to separate Stevie and Jeff. "Stop wrestling in the living room. You know you're not allowed to do this. Get up before I call Daddy at work."

"You're not the boss of me," said Jeff, slowly standing.

"Yeah," added Stevie, still clinging to both of Jeff's ankles. "You're just a kid, right, Jeff?"

Bending down, Collette yanked Stevie to his feet.

"Well I'm the oldest kid, which makes me more than *just* a kid."

"I am so bored," grumbled Jeff as he walked to the couch. "And I'm starving to death. When's Mom coming home? I have to be at soccer by five."

"My poor Bill is hungry, too," added Mrs. Withers. She took off her hat, examined it, and put it back on her head.

The doorbell rang as the keys jiggled in the lock.

"I hear Mommy," cried Laura, hopping off the couch and running to the front door. "She's using the front door, just like company."

Mrs. Withers stood up, examining her watch with great care.

"Come on in, Mommy," cried Laura. She pulled Mother in with both hands.

Mother flinched. "Ooooh, honey. Watch my sore fingers."

"Let me see," cried Stevie, racing across the room.

"See? The nurse at school put medicine on the burn and wrapped it in a big white bandage for me."

Mother extended her good hand toward Mrs. Withers.

"Mrs. Withers, I am so sorry to be this late. I did try to call twice, but the line was busy. . . ."

"My bear is upstairs talking to another bear," explained Stevie. "He won't hang up."

Mother sighed. "Oh, Stevie. You know you're not allowed to play with the phone."

"I know that, but my bear doesn't," mumbled Stevie.

"Anyway, I'm here now. I dropped my car keys down the sewer grate outside the school. This bandage is really awkward."

"How did you get home, Mom?" asked Jeff. "Did you hitchhike?"

Mother laughed. "No. I called the automobile club and they sent a man over to get the keys. But I ended up waiting over thirty minutes for his truck."

Mother paused to catch her breath. She sat on the couch and kicked off both shoes. "My feet are killing me."

Mrs. Withers cleared her throat like she was about to sing. "I better run, Mrs. Murphy. I already missed one bus, and my poor Bill is probably near death with hunger."

Collette handed Mother her purse. The sooner Mrs. Withers caught her bus, the better. She wasn't one bit worried about Mrs. Murphy's day. All she cared about was fixing food for poor Bill.

Mother fished through her wallet.

"Thanks for helping me out this week, Mrs. Withers. The children and I really appreciated it."

Mrs. Withers rolled up the money and stuck it in a small change purse.

"Except for you being so terribly late today, things weren't so bad. Will you be wanting me to come full-time in January?"

Mother swung both feet up onto the couch.

"Oh, I can't even think about all that now. I feel as though I have just jogged across the desert."

"Good-bye, then," said Mrs. Withers faintly as she opened and closed the door.

As soon as Mrs. Withers was down the walk, Laura reached for Mother's purse.

"Did you bring me my pink gum?"

Stevie raced across the room, rolling on top of Mother, "Yeah, and did you bring me some corn curls?"

Mother groaned. "Sorry, guys. I completely forgot."

"No fair," cried Stevie. "I was good for nothing."

Collette picked up Mother's purse and handed Laura and Stevie both a dime.

"Maybe Daddy can walk you both down to Marcus's when he gets home from work. Then you can pick out your own treat."

Jeff stood up and stretched. "Hey, Mom. Soccer starts at five. Chris said he could pick me up."

Laura sat up straighter. "Yeah, and I have my first Brownie meeting at six. Mrs. Hughes wants to know if you can drive, 'cause Matt will be asleep."

162

Mother covered her eyes and shook her head.

"And I was planning on staying on this couch till spring."

Mother stuck both feet back into her shoes and stood up.

"I guess if I start the hamburgers now, we just might make it."

"Where's my soccer shirt?" called Jeff as he raced up the stairs. "And I need white socks."

"Look in your top drawer."

Collette reached out and patted Mother on the arm.

"Thanks for letting my P.J.'s end up in the lost and found."

Mother grinned. "How would your teacher know what kind of baby-doll bottoms you wore? . . . I picked them up after school."

Mother opened the refrigerator, moving milk and juice around. Shaking her head, she opened the freezer.

"Oh, great. Mrs. Withers forgot to take the hamburger out of the freezer. It's as hard as a rock."

"I don't like rocks," said Stevie. "But my friend David likes mud."

Mother slumped into a chair. "Well, this is an

absolutely perfect ending to a hectic day. First the fire, then the dropped car keys, and now we don't even have a dinner. I certainly know how to make a mess of things."

Collette sat down next to her mother. "Mom, it wasn't your fault about the fire or the keys. And the fire turned out to be interesting. I doubt if anyone in my class will ever forget that science experiment."

"I don't know," sighed Mother. She rubbed her good hand over her eyes. "I was thinking on the way home that you were right after all, Collette. My job is being a mother, a full-time mother. I tried to do too much and I ended up not doing anything well."

"Are you real sad, Mommy?" asked Stevie. He leaned his head on Mother's lap.

Mother patted his head and smiled. It was a real tired smile.

In a second, Collette was up and out of her chair. She opened a cabinet and took out a stack of dinner plates.

"Get out the forks, Stevie," she said.

"Collette, what are you going to put on the plates?" asked Mother.

Collette swung open the refrigerator door, pulling out eggs and milk. With a tiny kick she closed the door with her foot.

"Stevie and I are going to make dinner, tonight. Is that okay with you, Stevie?"

"Ya-hoo," cried Stevie, dropping the forks on the table. He pulled open the lower bread drawer and climbed up on the counter. "Can I crack some of those eggs?"

Mother started to laugh.

"What are we having?" she asked.

"French toast," announced Collette. She reached under the cabinet and pulled out the metal griddle.

Stevie banged his spoon against the sides of the large red bowl. "I'm all ready, Collette."

"What do you want me to do?" asked Mother. She was sitting up straighter now and her smile looked happy.

Collette handed Stevie an egg and turned to grin back at her mother.

"Go in the living room and relax. I'm old enough to fix dinner."

"I guess you are," laughed Mother. "Wow — sitting all by myself in the living room. I won't know how to act with nothing to do."

"You can color in my robot coloring book," offered Stevie.

"Or you can think about that job offer, Mom."

Mother shuddered and made a sour face. "After today I'd rather not."

"Awful things won't happen every day," insisted Collette. "And even when awful things were happening around you, you didn't panic. You acted like a real teacher."

Mother groaned.

"I mean you *are* a real teacher," laughed Collette quickly. "Believe me, Mom. You were good. The whole class thought so . . . especially me."

Mother looked up and smiled.

"Thanks, Honey. It really means a lot to me to have your vote of confidence."

"I'll vote for you, too," added Stevie.

Mother got out of her chair real fast and hugged Collette and Stevie, the big red bowl in the middle.

"Hey," cried Stevie, sneaking out under Mother's arm. "Let's stop this hugging and start cracking some eggs."

Mother was almost out the kitchen when Collette remembered Roger's fossil.

Reaching into her pocket she pulled out the small square box.

"Roger asked me to give this to you . . . kind of like a going-away present."

When the box was open, Mother held up the small brown stone. "Look . . . see the fern imprint? What a thoughtful present."

"Roger must think you're real good," said Stevie, crushing another egg with his fist.

"She is," said Collette. She watched her mother studying the fossil as she walked down the hall.

"But she's the goodest mommy, right, Collette?"

"Right. Being our mommy is her favorite job. But if Mom wants to be a teacher for a while, then we have to let her know we won't be mad or sad. Okay, Stevie?"

Stevie dropped his spoon onto the counter, frowning.

"I will too be sad."

"But we can make it kind of fun, Stevie. I'll teach you all sorts of things to help out. We can even make an apple pie together."

Stevie's eyes brightened for a second before his chin shot out. He shook his head and pushed the large red bowl away.

"No. Let Mrs. Whiskers be the teacher and Mommy can be the mommy."

Collette pulled the bowl back in front of her and handed Stevie a measuring cup filled with milk.

"Pour all this in the bowl. Good . . . anyway, Mom still doesn't know if she's going to take the job or not."

Stevie looked up and grinned. "It's a secret, right, Collette?"

"Right."

Collette handed Stevie a slice of bread. "Now get this all wet in the bowl. You're doing a great job."

She lifted the soggy bread with the spatula, dripping a trail to the hot griddle.

As soon as Stevie heard the bread begin to sizzle and saw the tiny butter beads sliding across the griddle, he started to clap.

"Look, Collette! We did it. It's going to work!"

Collette took a proud poke at the bread with her spatula and smiled back.

"You're right, Stevie. It is!"

DATE DUE

OCT 1 1 2004			
			Printed in USA